D0364207

13	14	15	16	17
PROFESSION OR OCCUPATION	Employer, Worker, or Own account	If Working at Home	WHERE BORN	If (1) Deaf and Dumb (2) Blind (3) Lunatic (4) Imbecile, feeble-minded
School			France (French Subject)	X
...sor of Languages				
...ysician & Surgeon	own account	at home	Ireland	X
			India	X
...neral Serv. (Domestic)			London - Chelsea	
...tal Surgeon	do	do	do - St. James	
			do Bloomsbury	
...tis's Companion Dom			do Dalston	
...neral Serv. (Domestic)			Dorset - Sydling St Nicholas	X
...radise maker Dress	W	do	Ireland	X
			do	X
...do Dress	W		do	X
...ing on own means			Norfolk - Quinton Park	X
...treet messenger Port	Worker		London - Pimlico	
			do - Hammersmith	
			do - Kensington	
...ing on own means			Germany (Subject)	X
			Lancs - Liverpool	X
			London	
...ressmaker	own account	at home	Suffolk - Stowmarket	X
...ist 66	Worker		London - Kensington	
...tary Public Company	Employer		do - Marylebone	
...usekeeper (Domestic)			do	
...neral Serv. do			Jersey	X
...ssenger	Worker		Kent - Tonbridge	X
			London - St Pancras	
...illiker	do		do - Islington	
...erin in watch Co.			Middlesex - Harlesden	X
...do General Clerk Marine			London - Hammersmith	
			do do	
...uilder	W		do - Kensington	

1901 Census

PYRIGHT - NOT TO BE REPRODUCED WITHOUT PERMISSION

CM SCALE	1	2	3	4	5	6

THE HOUSE
IN LITTLE CHELSEA

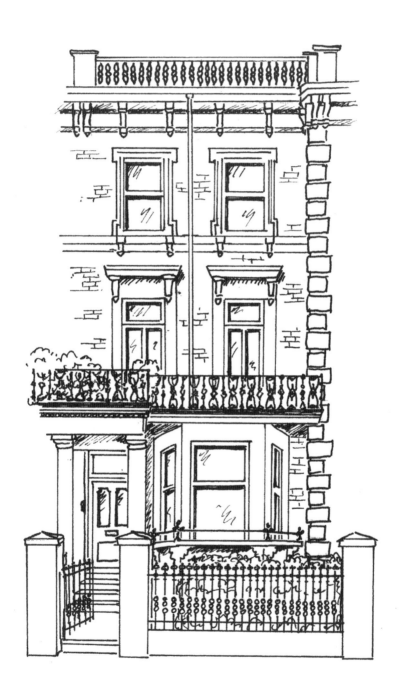

THE HOUSE
IN LITTLE CHELSEA

CLARE HASTINGS

PIMPERNEL
PRESS LTD
www.pimpernelpress.com

To Nick

Pimpernel Press Limited

www.pimpernelpress.com

The House in Little Chelsea
© Pimpernel Press Limited 2018
Text © Clare Hastings 2018
Design and illustration by Becky Clarke Design

Clare Hastings has asserted her right to be identified as the
author of this work in accordance with the Copyright, Designs
and Patents Act 1988 (UK).

All rights reserved. No part of this publication may be
reproduced, stored in a retrieval system or transmitted, in any
form, or by any means, electronic, mechanical, photocopying,
recording or otherwise, without prior permission in writing
from the publisher or a licence permitting restricted copying.
In the United Kingdom such licences are issued by the
Copyright Licensing Agency, Barnard's Inn, 86 Fetter Lane,
London EC4A 1EN.

A catalogue record for this book is available from the
British Library.

Typeset in Bembo

ISBN 978-1-910258-96-5
Printed and bound in China
by C&C Offset Printing Company Limited

9 8 7 6 5 4 3 2 1

CONTENTS

THE HOUSE 2017

A middle-class house, for a middle-class family. Part of a terrace of six symmetrical houses, set slightly back from the road. A flower bed sitting over a coal cellar combines with the metal railings and gate that front the property to give it a sense of enclosure, protecting it from the busy street. The gate also has a lock, to ward off undesirables. On the first floor is a balcony, edged with ornate black ironwork. The front elevation originally sported a masonry balustrade, now long gone, crumbled away from exposure to the elements. Steps lead you up to the front door, which is set back from a pair of pillars. There is a back garden – no more than 6 by 5 metres, but in this city a private outside space is gold.

The house is smaller than those built on the parallel street. Maybe the architects already had an inkling that it would not retain an air of gentility for very long.

It was substantially built, by the firm of Corbett and McClymont, who had already made their mark in The Boltons and Tregunter Road. They were modern builders in their day, and the house roof is of particular note, as it is set on bowstring trusses, so the weight of the roof is distributed to the walls, allowing for flexibility in the layout of the rooms. Inside there is a staircase taking you up through the house, and the drawing room has a high ceiling with an ornate cornice.

The house sits in an unpromising location, and there are few trees to break up the long street, yet it is a very London house, solid and of its period. It is a house that has known life. A lot of life.

Since the building was 'topped out' in 1873 more than seventy people have lived in this house. Children have been born in the rooms, but, rather strangely, it seems nobody has died there; however, this may be a natural result of the regularity of the changeovers. The house wears its cares lightly.

The house has witnessed a great deal of social change over its life. Gas lights have given way to electricity, horses to the motor car, and the once all-invasive fog of London has all but disappeared.

The nearby Ifield Road, once disrespected and down at heel, has become a 'go to' address, while Finborough Road, built to gentrify the area, has gained notoriety as an area of multiple occupancies. Everyone knows someone who has lived on the street, usually for the shortest possible time. Maybe it is that aspect of the street that makes for interesting living. A hop from some of the richest real estate in town, this house is so very London. A melting pot.

This is the story of some of the people who lived in the house. Their characters are imagined, but their names, ages and professions, provided by the census records, are all real. Their footsteps are etched into the floorboards, and their hopes, frustrations and happinesses are locked forever into the history of the house.

This is for them.

THE OCCUPANTS OF №.53

1873–1880
Edward Golding, 36 years; partner in a City law firm
His wife, Jane, 26 years
Three servants

1880–1891
William H. Amery, 55 years; bookseller (unemployed)
His wife, Hannah, 58 years

LETTING ROOMS TO:
Hildebrand Moore, 28 years; Irish barrister (unemployed)
Ada Reeve, 24 years; private means
Thomas Hartley, 45 years; William's widowed Scottish
    brother-in-law, hosiery manufacturer
One servant, maid-of-all work, Frances Holt, 25 years

1891–1893
William Holier, 59 years; engaged in interest of money and
    house property
His wife, Sarah, 54 years

1893–1901
David Robinson, 25 years; bank clerk

1901–1907
Geoffrey Harbird, 41 years; independent means supplemented
    by letting rooms
His wife, Ellen, 39 years
John Taylor, 15 years, Ellen's son; district post messenger
Maud Taylor, 13 years, Ellen's daughter

Annie Walsh, 38 years; widow and dressmaker
Olive Walsh, 15 years; Annie's daughter, typist
Moira O'Hull, 31 years; bodice-maker
Mary O'Hull, 26 years; Moira's sister, bodice-maker
Nellie O'Hull, 21 years; sister to Moira and Mary, bodice-maker
Esthanie Newman, 72 years; widow, living by own means
Joseph Newman, 38 years; Esthanie's son, assistant square-keeper
Kipper Newman, 37 years; Esthanie's daughter

1907–1919
Albert Arthur Warmbath, 42 years; chiropodist

LETTING THREE ROOMS TO:
Arthur Hagley, 40 years; motor cleaner and washer
His wife, Rose, 43 years
Their son Arthur, 16 years; motor tyre repairer
Their daughter Rose, 11 years
Their daughter Norah, 9 years
Their son Edward, 5 years
AND THREE ROOMS TO:
Jane Wood, 42 years; dressmaker

1920–1924
Corliss Claflin, 50 years; theatrical agent
His wife, Marnie, 46 years

The 1931 census records were destroyed in a fire. Census records ceased entirely during the Second World War and did not resume until 1952. So, effectively, from the 1920s to the early 1950s records were pretty much non-existent.

In the 1950s the house was occupied by Miss Dolby, followed by Mrs Keane, and in the 1960s by Hazel Adair, scriptwriter (*Crossroads*).

THE BUILDERS

SPRING 1873

WILLIAM CORBETT
Director of Corbett and McClymont, Builders

I am sick of banks. Rather, I am sick of visiting them. Today I did the rounds of three, securing further loans at variable rates. By a stroke of brilliance I offered the manager at The National Bank free use of a house at Westgate over Christmas, which certainly sweetened the pudding.

It has been a mixed day. On the good side I have just released the keys to no. 53 Finborough Road, which means that all my completed houses are now leased.

I had hoped to attract a slightly more affluent class to the road, and certainly the northern end of the street has been much slower to sell than the properties further down, but sell them I have, which should ease cash flow somewhat. I am determined not to relinquish the building standards for which our firm is famous. If we must pay more for better bricks, then pay we will. I seem to have reverted to the role of accountant, to leave McClymont (Alexander) to handle the day-to-day building. I used to enjoy watching the practical and the design side of building, but raising money is what I am good at, and also what we seem to need. The interest eats into profits. I am not interested in the selling process, so I am leaving that in the capable hands of Rogers and Chapman (Gloucester Road office), whose eyes positively glitter when a prospective client walks through their doors.

I am giving a dinner tonight for Lady Price, who looks good for investment. Our timber merchant, Alfred Waterman, has also expressed an interest in lending us funds. Alfred is much tickled by the idea that not only does he sell us the timber, but he also takes a share in the finished product. He is never happier than when we talk about the new steam-powered machinery he helped us to buy and install in the Lillie Road joinery shop. We have shared many an hour in the club discussing new methods of building, and myriad ways to use more product! He is fixated on the idea of timbered roads. I have pointed out that the horses' hooves may slip in the wet, but he is not be shifted, and indeed sees a sideline in specialist shoes. He is a man on a mission. But then, so am I.

Alexander came round to the office this afternoon. The masons have been stirred up by union talk from their 'brothers in the North': the joiners want grinding money, the painters want lodgings money and various overtime privileges that will not enhance our bottom line at all. They particularly object to hourly pay and want to be paid a day rate. They threaten to strike. I despair. Let them have my job, and they would see that there is a lot more to building a house than bricks and mortar. Alexander wants me to talk to the men and use my powers of persuasion, or work will grind to a halt. I will have to cancel several valuable meetings. I couldn't give anyone the real reason for my cancellations as I do not want funds to dry up – although I expect word will be out soon enough. I am absolutely resolute that I shall not pay a set rate. I will start out tomorrow and deal with the joiners. Grinding money, ha!

FIRST OVER THE THRESHOLD

THE NEWLY-WEDS
SPRING 1873

JANE GOLDING NÉE JOHNSON
Aged twenty-six years

Edward has collected the key to our very own front door. He is as thrilled as I am, although fearful that we may have paid too much. Luckily, finance is not on the list today. We are the first people to cross the threshold. Our very own brand-new house in Chelsea (the map actually refers to our area as ' Little' Chelsea, but it will always be just plain 'Chelsea' to me). Edward is going to be commuting to his office in Cannon Street, and I am to be left in charge, mistress of all things.

The very first thing I shall be doing is making a list of new furnishings. Edward thinks we can make do with the various trimmings provided by my mother, and some rather awful pieces provided by his (including a hideous sideboard which is much too large for the house), but he has made it quite clear that this is going to be my department, and I fully intend to run wild.

The move has taken a bit of time coming. We have been residing with my parents, who, though pleased to have us (well, me, at any rate), waved us off rather too cheerily, I thought. Edward has recently been made a partner at Gillett, Gosport and Ray, and is to be specializing in cases brought before the Court of Chancery. This is excellent news, as he tells me the cases run on forever, which means we will be in funds and I won't have to be too frugal when it comes to hiring staff and choosing materials.

I'm delighted to say Edward is quite a man of ambition (my sister's husband, John, being the complete opposite). He has taken to reading passages from a stirring self-help book by Samuel Smiles, which comes 'complete with illustrations', and it has really fired him up. He is now up on his feet and running. The new house is our first step into home ownership, and who knows what we may eventually aspire to – semi-detached, bay windows, a conservatory – but I am getting ahead of myself.

Edward has warned me to be wary of callers. At a quick glance it seems that our side of the street is inhabited by very respectable people – similar to ourselves. I have already been greeted by a slightly deaf colonel who lives only two doors down and I know that our architect (how grand that sounds) lives with his parents further up the street at no. 12. Edward is, however, more concerned about the inhabitants of Ifield Road. They are apparently a motley bunch, and the houses will not be home to anyone of influence, in fact probably the reverse. I have been instructed to turn left as I leave the house and not to cross over unless I have to. Well, the road is very busy, so this will not cause me any hardship. According to my brother-in-law John, there are several public houses locally. He assures me they are much further down the street and I certainly do not expect our neighbours will be frequent visitors to those establishments. How John is so familiar with them I can only hazard.

Our house has a certain grandness. We are set just back from the street, behind railings and a gate, which does much to enhance the appearance of the front. The pillars definitely give the property an allure. I'm not saying that we can compare ourselves to the houses over in The Boltons, but I certainly feel we have arrived somewhere, and somewhere is several steps up from my mother's spare bedroom.

EDWARD GOLDING
Aged thirty-six years, partner in a City law firm
Husband to JANE

What a relief finally to have our own house. Of course I am grateful to Jane's parents for their hospitality, but, oh goodness, those nightly lectures from her papa: 'Jane should not be expected to do this, or that or the other.' He must have fellow guests at his club snoring into the soup. I know I was in a perpetually glazed state most evenings. It was positively light relief to leave the table and go back into the drawing room to sit with her mama.

Jane is a different person when she is with me alone. With her parents present, she becomes quite retiring and shy, but then her mama is mistress of the quiet put-down. Mama was struck dumb when, over dinner last month, I quietly slipped into the conversation that I had been made partner and was now in a financial position to purchase our own home, and that her daughter would soon be running her own household. I would have given several of my hard-earned pennies to have captured a daguerreotype of her stunned expression.

I have had my eye for some time on a recently completed property in Little Chelsea. It has all the features you would expect of a design from the firm of Corbett and McClymont. I am most impressed with the way they move with the times, employing all the latest methods of build. The roof design particularly arrested my attention (Jane's less so). It is made apparently with a rain-resistant membrane − which seemed so obvious once they had pointed it out. They have been building properties all over the area, and have an excellent reputation, although I believe they are having a few disputes with their workforce over wages (what else?), and a strike is looming.

Luckily that doesn't affect us, as our house is finished and we will be in before the stucco is dry. We are both thrilled to have a brand-new house. There is something about being the first couple into a property that excites me. I intend to carry Jane over the threshold (although not up the front steps, as I don't want to court disaster in front of our new neighbours). The road is a busy one, but we both rather enjoy the bustle of traffic, and I feel certain that, as we are a property on the very border of Greater Chelsea, it won't be long before we are attracting a very good class of person to our new neighbourhood, and we shall be the front-runners. Ifield Road is a little down at heel (well, very down at heel really), but maybe Corbett can turn his attention shortly to that street and my investment will prove sound. John (Jane's brother-in-law) cast a sour note by mentioning he had seen in the papers a similar property for sale up the road a hundred pounds cheaper, and he thought we had paid somewhat over the odds (£530). I did not allow this to upset me (although I have to confess to a couple of somewhat restless nights), as by the time he was waving the property page in front of me I had already put down the deposit.

It is only money! I feel our future is now secure with the purchase of our new home, and when I turn the key to the door for the first time, I shall do so with a song not only in my heart but probably out loud too.

JANE GOLDING

It is not that I am a prude, far from it, but I do think there is a time and place to discuss plumbing. It is not at 10.30 a.m. on a Tuesday morning, when I am just getting ready to go out.

It is also not in front of our new maid, Jessie, who I caught sight of in the hall mirror laughing into her apron. I was just on the verge of opening the door to leave the house, when who should pound up the steps but brother-in-law John. He didn't wait to be asked in, but walked straight past me into the parlour, and sat down without even noticing I was wearing my pelisse and hat ready for the off. Anyway it turned out he is now a regular at the Finborough Arms up the road. He has a new drinking companion, Mr Thomas Crapper. It appears Mr Crapper likes to start his day with a refreshing bottle of champagne, and John is just the man to share it with him. This has evidently been going on for some time and they are now joined at the hip. How my sister puts up with it I do not know. Mr Crapper owns a plumbing business, and has apparently offered John a discount on his sanitary ware, including fitting the new 'Waste Water Preventer'. Not having his own home (I wonder why?), John thought to pass this arrangement on to us.

I hardly knew where to put myself. Luckily I was already seated. John said as I was already dressed to go out, why didn't we do a turn by Mr Crapper's Marlborough Road showroom, where we could see the wares comprehensively displayed in the window! I could only reply that I thought this to be more Edward's sphere than mine, and maybe he could call back one evening to discuss. John seemed quite put out, and said something to the effect that 'offers like that one don't come every day', and we should 'seize the moment'. It was only by promising to mention it to Edward at the first opportunity that evening that I managed to extract him from the house. I could hear Jessie downstairs chortling. Presumably telling Cook.

EDWARD GOLDING

Is a man to have no peace? I had barely walked through the door, and taken my hat off when Jane came bustling into the hall in an agitated state. It turns out that John has his eyes set on refurbishing our water systems, or rather his friend Mr Crapper has. I am perfectly content with the water closets we do have (why I am even thinking about this?) and I am not going to enter a discussion on the subject with poor Jane, who explained that she has been having a difficult day with the servants, who having overheard the earlier conversation have been living off it ever since.

Really, John is a menace. Not only will I have to put a stop to his sanitary ambitions, but I will also have to explain that some conversations are better off conducted between men, outside of the home. How on earth did he think he could take Jane to visit a plumber's showroom?

Of all the pubs in all the world, why on earth has he chosen to become a regular at the Finborough Arms?

JOHN EDMUNDS
Brother-in-law to JANE GOLDING

Edward and Jane have become house bores. They have already paid too much for the property — I told Edward as much before they moved in — and now seem determined not to take advantage of my connections to improve the facilities. I asked Edward to come down to the Finborough one morning and meet Thomas, but apparently the courts call, and he has no time off.

I have already made acquaintance with several of their neighbours, including Arthur Hughes, who is considered a painter and illustrator of note and married to the delightful (and very beautiful) Tryphena, who is also his muse. In turn they are friends with the Reverend Charles Dodgson, a regular visitor. Edward and Jane have no idea of the quality that resides a stone's throw from their front door. I shan't introduce them. Anyway, I can't see Jane posing as one of Hughes's wistful Ophelias. Jane thinks herself a step above her sister, Elizabeth (who would be more than happy with an outing to Crapper's), so I intend to keep any new discoveries to myself. The area is awash with types of humour and talent, but I can see they won't be heading towards no. 53.

EDWARD GOLDING

I can't believe it. I was late back tonight, due to a traffic jam involving a horse, two dogs and a drunken post-boy. I was just off the omnibus, and relieved to be making my way down the road home, when a particularly smart hansom stopped just in front of me, and disgorged brother-in-law John in full evening dress. I was in two minds whether to greet him, when he turned back towards the cab and helped a very svelte and elegant Elizabeth to negotiate the step. They looked so in the fashion, that I found myself shrinking into the shadows and actually putting my head down. John offered Elizabeth his arm and the two of them turned into the gate of no. 2. They were very lively up the steps and as the door opened, on the pretence of attaching a boot button, I managed to glance up. It was particularly galling to see the house absolutely twinkling, ready for what could only be a dinner party, and I swear I could hear the tuning up of a violin in the background. As they were whisked inside, just as the door was closing, John turned round. I feel sure he saw me − left out in the cold, so to speak.

I am stunned and mortified. It is not that I mind that our neighbours down the street have not been to call (surely John has mentioned us?), we have after all only been here a couple of months. It is that John has made absolutely no reference to the fact that he has any acquaintances living on the road, let alone smart ones. Did he see me? I so hope not, otherwise he will wonder what on earth I was doing skulking and avoiding them. He is bound to make a joke of it, and I will look a fool.

I won't mention it to Jane − but then if she finds out later it will be all over for me. John and Elizabeth live nowhere near here − for goodness' sake, they have lodgings in North London! I had assumed that Crapper and the Finborough were a passing amusement, and that he would soon be back to his old stomping grounds. But then I have observed that John has a way of getting to know people. They are drawn to his enthusiasms. So far we have enjoyed a sherry with the deaf colonel who lives two doors down, and Jane has received a card from our architect. It is hardly the cutting edge of society. I usually turn into our gate with a skip, but tonight I felt decidedly cast down. Silly, I know.

JOHN EDMUNDS

I do enjoy going to Finborough Road, and had the most delicious dinner with the Hugheses this week. Elizabeth was a huge success and has a new friend in Tryphena. They are planning no end of outings, and Tryphena insisted on giving Elizabeth a particularly decorative shawl she was wearing, as 'it is always colder in the North'. I wasn't sure where she thought we were going, but Elizabeth was enchanted, and talked about her new friend all the way home.

The funniest thing happened just as we were entering their house. Hearing a noise in the road, I glanced round – and there was Edward, looking decidedly ill at ease, bending over and fiddling with his boots. He must have seen us, as we were both quite animated on leaving the cab. I can only conclude he was avoiding us. I will allow him to think he has got away with it, and then in a couple of weeks' time, when I next go round, I will casually drop it into the conversation. Teasing Edward and Jane is the best of sports. I know I shouldn't, Jane being Elizabeth's sister and all, but I can't help it. They do so like to do everything by the book, which I suppose, given Edward's calling, is not surprising.

EDWARD GOLDING

I think I have got away with my extraordinary lapse in judgement last week. We have heard nothing from John, so I can relax. I had to tell Jane, who was much more agitated by the fact that we hadn't been invited to the party than by my embarrassment. I got a lecture on the need to be more active socially, and that I couldn't 'leave it all up to her'. I replied rather ill-naturedly that if all she could conjure up was a deaf colonel, then clearly I couldn't.

Thank you, John. Jane and I never have words, but he has sowed the seeds of social unease.

JANE GOLDING

It really is too irritating. John and Elizabeth have not even got a home to call their own, but they seem to be continually asked to other people's. I have been a bit tardy in taking round cards, but the truth is I have had such a lot on my plate that I haven't had a moment. It is top of my list today. I must say that running a house does seem to take up more time than I envisaged, and I haven't even started on the redecoration. Edward does not seem to grasp what is involved in running an establishment. I am still getting to grips with Cook and Jessie, who seem more intent on getting to grips with me than on running a tight ship downstairs. When we run through the menus, I see Cook giving me what can only be described as a 'look'. It is very unsettling, and sends me to asking a question as to the suitability of a certain mousse or jelly. Goodness, Mama's cook stands wooden spoon at the ready when she approaches, and the kitchen is run in military fashion. I am glad Edward never ventures below stairs, he would be dismayed at the lack of order. I think Jessie is willing, but knows that I am somewhat at sea. The other day I heard her mention crossly to Cook that the ornaments 'takes some dusting'. I suppose she would rather we lived in a bare room with a sofa in the centre. She has family in Ifield Road. Mama told me to employ a maid from the country, but she was the first to answer the advertisement, and seemed confident. Too confident, I now think.

I am going to leave a card at no. 2, where Edward spotted John and Elizabeth. The colonel has told me their name is Hughes. I shall not be left out, and I will not have Edward calling into question my visiting skills.

JOHN EDMUNDS

Elizabeth was at tea yesterday with Tryphena, when there was a knock on the door, and Jane's voice was heard in the hall. She had come to call. The maid came into the room bearing the card, and Jane was ushered in. It could have proved quite awkward, but Tryphena is a women who can handle any situation with tact, in fact she put Jane entirely at ease by putting the blame on herself for not calling first. Soon they were all chatting away, and Tryphena has promised to call on Jane in the next few days. I am glad they are all friends, for I would not wish the sisters to fall out.

I may have missed my moment with Edward. Still, I can rely on him to provide many more such occasions, I'm sure. Elizabeth tells me that Tryphena has asked her to pose for Hughes, who is planning a painting of the three muses. Elizabeth, Tryphena . . . as far as I can count that makes him one muse short . . .

EDWARD GOLDING

Came home to find Jane in high spirits. She took it on herself to call at no. 2. Apparently Elizabeth was already there, taking tea, but the lady of the house — Mrs Hughes — was delighted to meet Jane, and very apologetic for not having called on us first!

Jane tells me her husband is a painter of repute. Oh dear. I am not good with artistic types. They always seem to have me on the back foot. Mrs Hughes is apparently coming to give Jane help and advice with the furnishings. Apparently her house is 'decorated delightfully in the very latest colours'.

Why do I feel a frisson of unease?

JANE GOLDING

Mrs Hughes is no longer Mrs Hughes, but Tryphena. We are on first-name terms already! When I mentioned how much I had admired her drawing room, and that I was thinking of redecorating ours, Tryphena *literally* lit up. Apparently her favourite pastime is decoration, please, if she can be of any assistance, I only have to ask. So I have. I had been planning to visit Whiteleys, where I think there is good choice of papers, but, no, Tryphena says we must go Mortimer Street, where the showrooms stock papers of the highest artistic quality. She is personal friends with the proprietor at Jeffrey & Co., a Mr Warner. All their papers are arsenic-free, they have even won prizes for the quality of their work (and the lack of arsenic). We are going next Wednesday. In the meantime Tryphena has been looking around our house, firing off questions as we went into the rooms. 'Did I do *découpage*? What did I think of William Morris? Had we been to the Summer Exhibition?' All I kept saying was 'no', but she did not seem to mind or notice, so engrossed was she in picking up this and that, and peering into our closets. I am not sure Edward would like the idea of a relative stranger wandering round his dressing area and picking up his brushes, but I was helpless to deny her, following meekly round as though I were the visitor. By the time she had left we had totally rearranged the dining room and put in place ideas for a china room. Apparently Tryphena is an 'aesthetic' so we are only going to buy 'beautiful things'. I am to look for blue and white vases, and if I see a piece in 'ebonized wood' I am to reserve it and call on her immediately. I am so excited. I shall spend the whole week preparing for Wednesday.

I am to have a beautiful house in which to receive clever and amusing people. I shall need some new clothes. Tryphena has views on fashion as well. I cannot believe my good fortune. An 'aesthetic' and just down the road! (I must ask Edward what the word means.)

I have spent the week creating a *découpage* tray (I might well work my way up to a screen). I have been buying periodicals and cutting out pictures that appeal. Edward remarked that this was proving to be 'a very expensive tray'. I replied that you 'couldn't put a price on art', to which he replied yes, he could, as he was paying for the periodicals. I find the whole process very soothing and totally absorbing. Whole hours can pass while I decide whether to paste an illustration of a little dog, or a romantic ruin. I am becoming an aesthetic (I enquired of Edward as to the meaning of the word, rather wish I had not, as he is inclined to run on, but it boiled down to an appreciation of art, beauty and taste, all of which I can and will work on).

Jessie has cleared up all my scrap papers. They were in piles according to subject. Some have been torn and bent in the process. Surely she must have seen what I was doing! I called down to the kitchen and she popped up to be shown the damage. She looked me straight in the eye and said 'I know', to which I replied 'Well, that's all right then', upon which she turned round and went back downstairs. It was a very unsatisfactory encounter. Whenever Edward is home she bobs and nods as if her life depended on it.

On a happier note, a parcel arrive from Mama. While clearing out a trunk, she has discovered a small blue and white ginger jar. I had written alerting her to be on the lookout for *objets*. This will be the first pot of my new collection. I put it on the mantelpiece, and spent the rest of the day popping in and out of the room for a look.

—◦◦◦—

Wednesday. Tryphena was very impressed with my tray, and told me she thinks I may develop a discerning eye when it come to craft. She also spotted the ginger jar, and pronounced it 'charming', before taking it off the mantelpiece and putting it next to a group of glass on a side table. Apparently it was looking a bit lost. I have a lot to learn. She is loveliness itself.

I can see why her husband wishes to paint her. Even the way she leans against a chair is a study. Her jacket was black silk with bows and buttons pulling in her waist, the skirt dove grey trimmed with darker grey fringing and ribbons in the palest pink. The hat was the smallest I had ever seen and tilted at the prettiest angle. Her hair is a wonderful Titian red and dressed in twists and rolls that made my own efforts singularly uninteresting. Apparently the hat came from Paris! When I commented on her gown, she laughed and said, 'Oh, this old thing! It was designed by Messrs Swan and Edgar and I was thinking it a bit dull. How kind you are to notice.' Tryphena says I should only wear drab olive colours, to compliment my complexion, and had I been to see Worth? I said no, but I had read of him. Which I had — some of his designs forming part of my *découpage* tray, cut out from my *Ladies' Magazine of Fashion*. At this point Tryphena said we had better go, as Mr Warner at Jeffrey & Co., was expecting us and we didn't want to be too late. Just as we were gathering our things there was a knock on the door, and who should appear but John. I swear he must have rooms in this street! I was in the middle of telling him we were already late for an appointment, when Tryphena rested a hand lightly on his arm, saying, 'Do come with us, a man's opinion is always of interest, especially when it comes to choosing papers.' John is not a man to say no to any invitation and pronounced shopping to be his favourite pastime (he once told me how he felt an hour in a shop was an hour wasted), and he would go at once to secure a hansom for us. I felt a twinge of disappointment. It was to have been my outing.

EDWARD GOLDING

For the last week I have been used to coming home to find Jane engrossed in papering a tray — so engrossed that she hardly looks up when I come through the door. So tonight I was surprised to find her sitting in a chair with a book open on her lap, clearly unread. On my enquiring about the tray she gave a slight sigh, before coming over to give me a warm embrace. This was welcome, but unusual. As we went into dinner, the first thing I noticed was that a ginger jar (a present from her mama) had been relegated to a dark spot on a side table. Jane was nearly silent through the soup, and only toyed with a cutlet. My gentle probings as to what was the matter met with a dull silence, leaving me to ramble on about my day. It was soon pretty clear that I was talking to the wall and that Jane, apart from the occasional 'hmm' or 'really', was not concentrating on the finer points of my court appearances, but pondering on some disagreeable occurrence from earlier. In a flash of brilliance that would have impressed even a Sherlock Holmes, I asked about her day with Tryphena Hughes. I certainly hit the spot! She stood up from the table, said would I mind if she retired early, as she had 'a lot on her mind', and she would ask Jessie to clear when I had finished my cold shape. I had already finished with it, as it tasted mostly of flour, but I said nothing and let her leave the room quietly. I can see I will have to wait for her to come to me with her problem.

I took the opportunity to help myself to an extra sherry from the sideboard, and enjoy a quiet (and excellent) cigar. I had been given a box of very fine Havanas as a gift following the bankruptcy of Hollingsworth, a wine and spirits merchants who were also (until their demise) cigar dealers. I had hardly put leaf to lip, when Jane came back in. I knew I was in for a difficult hour when she opened the conversation with the words 'Oh Edward, I have had the most horrible day.'

—◦ΘΘΘ◦—

Well! I hardly knew what to say, except to agree that the day had indeed been horrible. Events seem to have evolved as follows (Jane has a habit of meandering when she speaks, but her delivery is lively). The trio had set off for Mortimer Street in a hansom. Jane had entered the cab first, followed by Mrs Hughes, with John squeezed in beside her. It quickly became clear to Jane that John's arrival had been not fortuitous but pre-planned, and the light-hearted conversation which they engaged in made it evident that they were used to spending time in each other's company.

Jane sat miserably through the journey, Mrs Hughes using the occasion for increasing familiarity between her and John, allowing him to help her out of the cab and into the shop, creating such an impression that the proprietor, a Mr Warner, said, 'Mr and Mrs Golding, delighted you could both come', which upon explanation caused much merriment amongst the three of them. Jane came forward and had to introduce herself, or 'it would have looked as if I had just walked in off the street'.

Then commenced the work of the day, choosing the papers for our home. John and Mrs Hughes leant forward to peruse the books together, actually whispering to each other and laughing when their hands touched as they turned the pages. Jane sat mute, 'for I could not see the book, and anyway felt that my opinion was neither sought nor needed.' Between the two of them it was decided we were to have Morris & Co. designs for both the dining room and parlour and plain colours in the bedrooms! Mr Warner told them they had excellent taste and the papers were the latest designs from the master, and would certainly be brightening up our dark corners. He also recommended a firm for painters and hangers. The orders were just going in the book, when Jane summoned up the strength to say she would need to think on it, and must consult with me before committing to the proposal. Everyone then went very quiet and they all turned to Jane. Mrs Hughes gave a slight smile. 'But, dear Jane, you asked me to help, and here I am giving up time to advise, as you asked. Mr Warner does not see just anybody. What would you have us do? Cancel the order?'

Apparently, unable to respond, Jane then got up, not looking at either of them, and requested from Mr Warner that he find her a hansom, which he promptly did. She arrived home alone, and has not spoken to anyone since.

Poor, dear Jane. At the worse she has been made complicit in some sort of friendship between Mrs Hughes and John, and at the best she has been made to look a fool by them. I am so angry, but it was not the time for rage but comfort. I blame myself too. I have been working too much, and putting Jane under pressure to run our first home. I have promised that I will go and speak with Mr Warner and at a suitable time we will go together to look at the papers, and select the ones that *we* like for *our* house.

The tale took some telling, longer than the envisaged hour, but it certainly kept my interest. I stopped Jane every now and again, as I wanted to marshal the facts. It is all in the detail. One thing is certain, I never want to see him in this house or hear of that dreadful woman again. I am always happy in the company of Jane, and would rather suffer a month of dinners with the deaf colonel than have her compromised and slighted. Indeed, as I said to Jane, I never could see a problem with any of our furniture, and was very attached to some of the pieces, particularly my mother's sideboard (a remark which, sadly, did not console her, but released a fresh trail of tears).

JANE GOLDING

Of course, it is true, I did ask Tryphena to help me with the decoration, and that makes me feel so foolish. I should have known that Tryphena was too worldly to find time with me anything other than a distraction. I cannot say anything to my sister. It would not end well. I think it is now fortunate that they do live in North London, as it does not require me to keep regular contact. Edward was kindness itself, and indeed seemed to find my account of the day as riveting as one of his cases, asking me to go over certain points several times and punctuating my tale of woe with questions. He hung on my every word, which in a funny way was quite exciting! He does not usually find my day so riveting. He has even offered to come with me to Jeffrey & Co. I know that he thinks the house is perfect as it is, which should be enough for me, but the fact is when it comes to fashions, he does not know his Swan from his Edgar. As for that hideous sideboard, it takes up the whole room, and his mama was thrilled when Edward professed an interest in it. I hope never to see John or Tryphena again, which I suppose is a vain hope given that one is my brother-in-law and the other a neighbour. I have learnt a valuable lesson and shall not be throwing myself so eagerly into future friendships (Mrs Beeton has written sage words on this very subject, I should have taken heed). Edward is going to see John (not here, thank goodness) and I think rather looks forward to the encounter. I can see why he was made a partner in the firm. I feel quite proud of him. I have never seen him so fired up before. It really was rather thrilling!

—⟨∞⟩—

I am quite recovered from last week, to the extent that Edward and I have invented a new parlour game. It is called 'Question and Answer', and it is a source of much excitement in the evenings. I spend the day making up a story. It can involve a cast of characters – or it could be all about me! Then Edward puts on his stern voice and 'cross-questions' me about the tale. I have to be very quick to think up answers to his questions and often I completely forget what or who I am talking about, at which point we both fall about laughing. Edward says it is now the high point to his day, and he can't wait to come home to see what tales I have for him. I am really becoming very inventive. Edward sometime stands up when he cross-questions me and paces up and down, hands behind his back as he walks. Other times he suddenly looms over me, to ask a question in such a loud voice that I tremble. Cook and Jessie must wonder what we are up to, as while before the game we were quite silent in the evenings, a book or cards being the night's entertainment, now we are falling all over the room. It really has brought a focus to our lives, and we sometimes find ourselves starting to play the game before breakfast. It makes me feel a real part of Edward's life, and I can see he feels the same. There is certainly a frisson to our marriage that was not there before.

I have not been feeling well. Yesterday evening we were enjoying a particularly merry session of 'Question and Answer'. I had spent the morning fashioning some handcuffs from a couple of bracelets and a length of grosgrain ribbon. Edward was pretending to 'take me down', and was fiercely rattling the handcuffs, when out of nowhere I came over quite faint, and had to sit down.

Edward brought me a glass of fortified wine to ease the dizziness, but I could not resume our game, and went to bed early. Then at breakfast Jessie had just placed a rather dismal plate of eggs and haddock in front of Edward, and I was waiting for my hot chocolate, when a strange and instant nausea came over me, not unlike the sickness I experienced once on the mechanical ride in Cremorne Gardens. I knew I was not happy with Cook's blancmange last night — it had a distinctly sour taste. But Edward had noticed nothing, and tucked down his morning haddock while I retired to loosen my corset, which I have noticed to be pinching slightly of late.

I do hope I am not sickening for something unpleasant.

—◦◦◦—

Jessie came up to bring me a tray to my room, as I did not feel like getting up for luncheon.

She placed the tray by the bed and, instead of retiring, hovered by the window, twitching at the curtains. This is usually her method of relaying to me that there is something on her mind.

Without looking round, she said, 'Madam, Cook and I have been wondering . . .' (then there was a long pause while she continued to shake the curtains) 'whether you might not have fallen?'

Sometimes I think she is a bit simple. I replied, rather tartly, that I had certainly not fallen, and I thought I would know if I had. In the meantime, if she could look to the cleaning of the cutlery, and tidy the china cupboard, I would be down after a short rest. (After she had gone I rather regretted the instruction, as china and Jessie are not a happy combination, and I now have only six saucers left from a set of ten that my mama gave us for a wedding gift. Still, I am not planning to have ten for tea this week, so I shall manage.)

I got up for the evening, and when Edward came home, thinking it would amuse him, I told him that Jessie and Cook are convinced I have taken a tumble, which has in turn brought on my sickness. Edward gave me a strange look, and asked me for Jessie's exact words. I told him that I wasn't playing the game.

He said neither was he. I repeated verbatim (one of Edward's favourite words) her phrase, even mimicking the shaking for the curtains, which I thought a good touch.

He gave me a long look and said, 'I think Jessie and Cook may be right. Have you thought that you might be expecting a child?'

The minute the words were out, I could not think why it had not occurred to me before. We celebrated with a sherry, and Edward enjoyed a Hollingsworth cigar, at which point I had to leave the room instantly. I hardly know what to feel. I lay in bed thinking of names for the infant, but as the night progressed my sleep was consumed with thoughts of a different nature – mostly, I am ashamed to admit, not about baby but about my mortality, which led me to making a list of prospective wives for Edward in the eventuality that I died during labour. These morbid thoughts did not make for a calm night.

No wonder my corsets have been feeling tight!

EDWARD GOLDING

I am to be a father. The very word fills me with excitement. I shall do everything I can to keep Jane happy and in health. We retired early, and I was sound asleep when suddenly I was dragged from my slumbers by the sound of Jane crying out fretfully in her sleep. She spoke quite clearly, each time mentioning a lady by name, 'NO, NOT Arabella Isley, WHAT, Victoria Swainston – IMPOSSIBLE. Merry Johnson? RIDICULOUS.' Even Mrs Hughes was mentioned – 'TRYPHENA – THEY WON'T MATCH!' this remark was accompanied by a flaying of her arms, as if warding her off. Finally she shouted out 'TOO TIGHT, TOO TIGHT!' And then she fell into a silence, and did not move until morning.

What can she have been dreaming of? Jane does not usually talk in her sleep. All the ladies were known to me, one of them a childhood friend whom I have not seen since I was in the nursery. I am surprised Jane even remembered her name. What can be preoccupying her? It was a fascinating insight into Jane's mind. I have decided to keep a pencil and paper by the bed and make some notes of any further sleep experiences. They may provide a valuable insight into the state of her health and that of the baby. I have always had an interest in dreams – now I can put this to practical purpose.

No expense spared. I have written to engage Dr Thomas, who lives close by on Redcliffe Square and attended Lady Wells at her confinement. I have also mentioned, in case it is of help to him, that I am noting down the substance of Jane's dreams. I am planning to buy a small pamphlet I have seen on the subject, which may help us understand her anxieties. I have told Jane about my intentions, but she was not as excited as I had hoped, caring more about the sickness that has taken her over. I said sagely, 'Understand the mind, Jane, dear, and you are more than halfway to solving any physical malaise', whereupon she went a strange shade of puce and left the room. I shall buy the pamphlet on the way home from work, then she will see what a useful tool this will prove to be in the coming weeks.

As soon as I had purchased the pamphlet Jane fell completely silent, and apart from the odd twitch or moan has not revealed anything of substance. So, after keeping myself awake for several nights, I feel inclined to move on. Included in the publication are several pages on the subject of moles. Jane has two moles, one on the side of her neck, and one on her left breast. The one on her neck signifies that she is going to narrowly escape suffocation, but will survive to receive an unexpected legacy; the one on her left breast shows sincerity in love, and an easy childbirth. Apart from the unpleasantness of a suffocation (which, as the pamphlet clearly states, is not fatal), the prognostics are excellent. I am thrilled with my new purchase. As Jane is retiring earlier now, I have plenty of time to study this fascinating subject. I have started to observe my work colleagues quite intently, to the extent that my clerk enquired the other day if he had done something amiss. 'Only the mole will tell!' I said enigmatically. It is difficult, as I am not in a position to see the marks on my clerk's body, but I could have told him that the one on his eye was troubling, denoting a steady disposition but meaning that in all probability he is likely to suffer a violent death. I can see this is the sort of information that weighs heavy on a man. I am not sleeping well.

JANE GOLDING

Dr Thomas came to see me. He is aware of all the latest techniques and, like our dear Queen, recommends chloroform be used during birth, which has taken a weight from my mind.

Apart from resting as much as possible during my confinement, I must eat plain but nourishing food to encourage regular bowel movements (I must talk to Cook, her recipes being more likely to induce the reverse effect), avoid alcohol, although a glass of beer is beneficial, and loosen my corsets. I have already ascertained that I can purchase a specially designed shape that will give me support, but allows for baby. I am in good health, and he will not need to see me again until the birth. I also have the name of a local midwife who will assist.

I mentioned Edward's new fascinations. He said that he too was interested in the analysis of the mind, but we had a long way to go in this area, and he was not convinced that Edward's book would provide all the answers. In the meantime he would look to the forceps and chloroform to ensure a safe and happy birth.

I felt much better for seeing him. He has a way that inspires confidence, although I did not need to see the forceps, which he had brought along to reassure me of his credentials. He kept opening and closing them to demonstrate their effectiveness. 'See, Mrs Golding, how they grasp baby's head. Just like taking a chicken from the oven. Snap, snap.' I am afraid I actually had to look away when he produced a book of anatomic drawings from his bag. I needed the beer when he had departed, and slept for the rest of the morning.

Edward has been sleeping badly. He tells me I have talking in my sleep – well, he has been positively shouting. I have found the pamphlet that he has been studying, hidden under a cushion in the parlour. This reveals two things. One, that Jessie has not been shaking the cushions properly; two, that Edward is taking his hobby very seriously. He has been marking in the margin the names of people at his office, and using a series of arrows and sketches to match their facial characteristics – the positioning of moles, the colour of their eyes, even their hairline – to the corresponding prognostics within the pages. He clearly hopes to gain an understanding as to the personality and fate of his acquaintance. In fact the pages are so awash with the pencil markings that it is hard to read what is underneath. I did see Jessie's name, but could not decipher which line the arrow pointed to. (Certainly not 'industrious' or 'will experience death by cleaning'.) I do not know what to think. It is unsettling to know I am being studied as I sleep, although now I have found the book I shall certainly listen more intently to Edward's nightly conversations, so I can make a more informed opinion as to the science behind it. This is something Edward is always challenging me to do. He does not approve of sloppy thinking. In the meantime I shall replace the pamphlet where I found it.

—⟋⟍⟋⟍⟋—

Edward's dreams are proving to be sadly lacklustre. I had hoped to open a window into the workings of an insightful mind, but he seems to dream in the mundane. None of his dreams seem to be referenced in the pamphlet. The first night he seemed to dwell mostly on Dr Thomas's bill, which had arrived that morning: 'How much? HOW MUCH?' – he repeated the words several times, each time his tone growing louder with agitation. Then he moved on to the office: 'I want you all to LINE UP and SHOW ME YOUR MOLES.' Obviously no one was responding, as he became quite cross. 'YES, you there. Your moles. NOW.' I could not put up with it any more and gave him a light shove to awaken him. He hardly noticed, but the talking ceased. Last night was no better, and concerned our neighbour, the deaf colonel. Edward's voice was raised to a shout: 'I SAID PASS THE SHAPE. THE SHAPE, MAN. THERE, THERE TO THE LEFT.' I have told Edward this cannot go on, and tonight gave him a liberal portion of my sleeping draught, which he watered down with sherry. He slept soundly.

EDWARD GOLDING

Clearly, carrying the weight of so much personal information concerning my friends and fellow-workers is taking its toll. Jane tells me I have been much disturbed in my sleep of late, which was not the point of the study. I may have to leave this new science to men of a more robust nature. It is a pity, as I really feel that I have something to contribute to this branch of medicine.

I am, however, not surprised that Dr Thomas's bill invaded my nightly rest. Jane tells me he was only here for half an hour, and much of that was spent showing her his medical equipment. As I am assuming it is not she who will be using it, I could see little point in filling up the time with a practical demonstration. I shall not question his bill, but I am grateful that Jane is well, and not taken to faints and vapours. Apparently there is no need for him to return until the end of her confinement. I had better start putting funds aside now, and hope for a quick delivery!

JANE GOLDING

We have been discussing names. Edward is convinced I am to have a boy, and has suggested Wilfred, after his father, or Stanley, after his grandfather. I said that maybe if I have a girl we could call her Rose, a name I have always loved. Edward agreed, but only because he is sure it will be a boy. This is due to my size. Edward says I am now as large and as heavy as one of Cook's suets. Apparently he was a large baby, weighing in at 11 pounds. This was not reassuring, but it is true I have been gaining a lot of late. Edward came home yesterday with a little box of lead soldiers, and spent the evening arranging them in rows, while I stitched away at a little cap I have been making. Mama has sent my old cradle, that she has been keeping for just this moment, complete with new sheets and pillow. I have embroidered a 'G' on the corner of each sheet. Jessie has been polishing the wood with beeswax and it shines like new.

The midwife, Mrs Meacher, has been to call. She appears tidy and efficient. Apparently it will not be long now. I am terrified, but will not give way to my fears. Mrs Meacher has administered the chloroform many times, and assures me as to its safety.

I can tell Edward is worried too, as he does not like to talk about the birth at all, and is happiest when sorting out the soldiers. Mama gave birth to three of us. My elder brother died at three months, but Mama remains fit and healthy, so there is no reason it will not be the same for me. Mrs Meacher tells me to plait my hair, as I may not be up to dressing it after the birth. I am glad she is so confident that I will survive, even if it is only to keep my hair brushed.

I slowly perambulated my way around Brompton Cemetery in the afternoon to get some exercise – being in the house so much is making me feel claustrophobic. But I cannot think what possessed me. The air was foul and gloomy and the stones seemed particularly poignant. I often walk around the grounds, and they had not struck me as such before. Next time I decide to go out, I shall choose Kensington Gardens. They are further away, but a walk around the Italian Garden always fills me with pleasure. Anyway, I am not supposed to leave the house. Jessie was quite relieved when I reappeared. As she is one of eight, she knows the signs of an imminent delivery. I went back upstairs to lie down. We will be in need of a new bed at this rate.

EDWARD GOLDING

A GIRL. Her name is Rose. She is perfect and Jane seems to be recovering splendidly.

I came home to find the house in a state of uproar, Jessie carrying pails of hot water up the stairs and all the signs that the good doctor had started to clock up his hours. Apparently Jane had been in labour since lunchtime, but the doctor had only arrived a few moments before I came in (seven o'clock). The midwife was at hand to administer the chloroform and there was nothing I could do except retire to the parlour. I told Cook that dinner could wait, not wanting to add to the unfolding drama. I had already had oysters in a pudding for luncheon, so was not in any hurry to eat.

It was very difficult to know how to pass the time. I kept getting up and down. First I stood at the bottom of the stairs, which made me look and feel rather foolish. I then thought to position myself outside the bedroom, but had to retire as I found the noises and activity most unsettling. Only by sorting the lead soldiers into battle order was I able to soothe my nerves. In the end I asked Cook if there was any chance of a savoury, as I needed a distraction. Then, just as she had assembled a couple of kidneys on some fried bread, I heard a cry from upstairs. I rushed up to be confronted by the doctor and Mrs Meacher, who said that I could go in for five minutes only, and then the mother must be left to rest. MOTHER! Dearest Jane was holding our little girl, and looking radiant. I have never been prouder or loved her more. I hardly had time to kiss and hold my family when Mrs Meacher appeared and I was removed from the room.

Dr Thomas was downstairs and clearing up his bag. Apparently everything has gone well. The next few days are critical, but he can see no cause for any concerns at the present. Baby Rose is a good weight and Jane lost little blood. But if either of them shows any sign of a fever he must be sent for immediately.

I opened a bottle of port to celebrate and gave Dr Thomas a Hollingsworth cigar from the box, which is getting rapidly depleted. He made as if to sit down, but, mindful of his hours, I said would it seem amiss if I bade him a speedy farewell, so I could write notes to the family to reassure them of Jane and baby's well-being. He seemed slightly put out, but shook my hand warmly and wished us well, instructing me again to make sure I called him straight away if I had any concerns. He then went out to what was a particularly dark and fog-filled night, but, as I said cheerily when I waved him off, he does not have far to go.

Going back inside, I feel that everything has changed. We are a family. I am a father. I collapsed into a chair to absorb my feelings, but such was the emotion of the moment that I fell straight into a slumber, only to wake as dawn came through the window, and I heard the small cries from my baby Rose as she too woke to start the day.

JANE GOLDING

We are to move. I feel as though we just arrived. Little Rose has become the centre of our world. There could not be a more loved child, which is the reason for leaving our house. Smallpox has broken out in Ifield Road. I have forbidden Jessie to visit her family — we cannot take any risk of the infection spreading to our street. I need not have bothered to tell her, she knows about the perilous effects already. If it were possible the fogs are becoming worse, I could not see across the road this morning and Rose has developed a slight cough. Edward went today to look at a villa in Hampstead, where we will be on higher ground with clean air.

Of course I will also be nearer to my sister and brother-in-law (whom I have not seen since the 'Tryphena affair'). Elizabeth has been to visit on several occasions, but is always rather vague when I ask about John, and I do not pursue it.

As it turned out, I did not need the forceps (I think just looking at them gave me the will to push, and Rose probably felt the same). Dr Thomas seemed rather disappointed. 'A natural mother, Mrs Golding, ah well, always another day, eh, Mrs Meacher?' He smiled, raising his eyebrows in a jovial way, as he packed them back into his bag with all the other hardware he had brought along 'just in case'. I think that humour in a doctor is much overrated.

Going Down

So Edward and Jane move from their first home to take up residence in the Vale of Health, Hampstead. Their chapter in the history of the house is over. It is also the start of a slide in the fortunes of the house, as it moves from the gentility of single-family ownership to the start of decades of multiple occupancy.

Brother-in-law John was right over one thing. It turned out they had paid too much for the house. The developers had overreached themselves, misjudging the markets and the type of individuals who would desire to reside in the properties. The Building News, *a stalwart publication of the time, reported that in South Kensington 'they have overbuilt', and that many properties were standing empty. The market collapsed. In 1878 Corbett and McClymont went into bankruptcy, the tipping point brought on by — of all places — St Luke's Church, Redcliffe Square. Wages, materials and the hazards of money-raising against a falling-off in demand for their properties combined to bring about their demise. Corbett himself blamed 'the terrible depression in property, which has happened not only to our estate, but also in the neighbourhood'. McClymont decided to the best way to recover from the collapse of the company was a visit to the boat race.*

In 1880 the key of the front door passes to one William Amery, a bookseller, and his wife, Hannah. Their finances require them to take in lodgers, and the rooms are taken by a Miss Ada Reeve, Hildebrand Moore, a barrister, and William's widowed brother-in-law, Thomas Hartley, who is a hosiery manufacturer. Times are hard, and they are all to be looked after by a maid-of-all-work, Frances Holt.

THE NEW KEYHOLDERS

THE BOOKSELLER
AUTUMN 1880

WILLIAM AMERY
Aged fifty-five years, bookseller

The book trade is not what it was. All anybody wants now are newspapers and magazines. Oh – and circulating libraries. I'd close them. Railway bookstalls – I'd close them too. Penny fiction. Penny dreadful! As it is, I've been closed – or, I should say, taken over. Mrs Amery says I should have diversified – cards, stationery, that sort of thing. But I am a book person, always have been.

You can tell a lot about a person by their books. I fancy now that I can tell what a customer will buy just by a look at them.

Some will favour books on science or philosophy, but you can tell by the way they handle them they won't be read, just titles to display and impress their friends. Some will buy a certain size and colour, maybe to furnish a library, and then order them by the yard like a pair of new curtains. Then there are the ones for whom there is this emotional connection. They pick up a book, and hardly dare to open it in case they mark it or crack the spine. You see them holding just the corner of a leaf with their fingertips as they gently turn the pristine pages. Others glance through the index, selecting first one chapter and then another at random, reading swiftly to see if the author can keep their attention.

To observe the delight that comes from paper and see the pleasure derived from the mere act of looking at words on a page is a privilege. Oh, and don't get me started on the smell! For me it's like a fine wine. I can tell the notes. The ink, the glue, the paper. Old books have different notes, as the chemical reaction in the paper changes over time to produce sweet odours. I have seen a man bury his nose in a book and inhale as though it were his lover. I understand that. Smell can be a warning too, of damp and mould, the enemy of the written word, and a breeding ground for the book lice that feast on it.

I have always wanted my own library. I said to Mrs Amery, if ever we move the first things I want to build are shelves. Shelves for books. My books would probably smell of tobacco and pipes.

I am an incessant smoker. Reading and smoking, smoking and reading, my favourite occupations. Anyway, that is not to be. It has not been a good year. We have lost the shop (lost – an odd word to apply to a failed business, as though I had carelessly mislaid it, leaving it behind, like my brolly in a coffee house), our home and our old way of living. We have now, in an effort to settle my debts, moved from some style in the West End to the borders of Little Chelsea. We are to give shelf room not to books, but to lodgers.

My sister succumbed to consumption, and we have 'adopted' Thomas, her husband, who is going to be sharing our home. I think he finds comfort from being with us, and he knows we are always ready to talk of her. He manufactures hosiery, and finds that trade as difficult as I do mine. Maybe we are just not good at business, but it is not for the want of trying. Thomas works long hours and is as committed to discussing stockings as I am books. We certainly make a peculiar couple.

I am going to sell the remainder of my stock from the house, using advertisements to secure clients and then posting the books out. I enjoy wrapping books. Whether a book is good or bad the one thing you can't alter is its shape, so it remains the easiest of parcels. When it is tied up, the string secured with a dab of red wax, I can never fail but reap satisfaction from this simple task well done.

Discounted books delivered by mail order. That is to be my future, so I had better get used to it.

HANNAH AMERY
Aged fifty-eight years
Wife to WILLIAM

I said to Mr Amery, what's wrong with a humorous card, or a nice box of writing paper? Everybody needs that. He could have sold pens too, or a pencil set. You can't rely just on books. Diversify, move with the times. Too late now. It is a relief to have settled the bills. It is not pleasant to wake every day to a new debt. Mr Amery blames the circulating library, the devil's work.

The house is solid, but part of a terrace. Sometimes you can hear the neighbours through the walls. I am used to servants, but now we are down to a maid-of-all-work, Frances. And we are to take in lodgers, needs must. Mr Amery put an advertisement in *The Times*. We had several replies, and selected two. Miss Ada Reeve, a secretary, and a Mr Hildebrand Moore, who is a barrister. Both had good references, and seemed polite and genteel. In fact, Mr Moore is rather the dandy, and I can see will be keeping us all up to the mark. Thomas, who is Mr Amery's brother-in-law, has come to lodge too, so we will be quite the merry band. I will have to help Frances in the kitchen or the dinner will never get done. Flour on the fingers will be an experience I have not had since I was a little girl, when Cook let me help with the biscuits.

The funniest thing — while I was sorting out a cupboard I came across a not-unattractive *découpage* tray and a blue and white china ginger jar, clearly left behind by the previous owners. I have brought them out, dusted them off and will put them on display in the dining room. The ginger jar looked quite at home on the mantelpiece. I found myself popping in and out during the afternoon to look at it. The house was completely cleared apart from those two pieces — it is strange what people leave behind.

I am sorry to say that I suspect mice. In fact I don't suspect, I know. I said to Mr Amery, we need a cat. I don't like them, but I like mice even less. He will look for one tomorrow. Our only extravagance is to be a bath. Our resources may be limited, but there is no reason not to move with the times. I said to Mr Amery, if it was good enough for the Romans, then I think we have waited long enough. Mr Crapper has a showroom down the road and he can supply and plumb. I felt cleaner as soon as the decision to install was made.

We are going to provide board as well as lodging. Breakfast and an evening meal, served at 6 p.m. We have enough furniture for all the rooms, but Thomas in particular wished to bring his own, which was no hardship for us. I will give each of them a key to their room and a set of rules. Not many, but I always think it is better to set out the parameters in advance and then there will no argument.

Mr Amery is to convert the parlour into a small office and sorting room, from where he can catalogue and marshal the orders for his new book business. I am pleased to sacrifice the room, as before that he was really very cast down. It affects a man to lose his work, and for Mr Amery his work was more of a calling than just a job. I am going to help him with the accounts this time. I am good with numbers. This afternoon we will organize the stock into boxes. Mr Amery says I am his little 'Amazon, The Warrior Queen of Books'. I was just copying out my list of house rules at the time so I made to joust at him with my pencil. At least we can still have a good laugh.

HILDEBRAND MOORE
Aged twenty-eight years, barrister

At the present time I am finding my fees disappointingly low. In fact, I am having to supplement my income by writing up crime reports. I am not the only one, there is quite a group of us now, but at least I am in court every day sucking up the atmosphere and listening to the arguments from some of our best legal minds. I chivvy up my clerk on a daily basis (when I can find him; he seems to make a habit of always being 'out'). I am lodging with Mr and Mrs Amery. Mr Amery is a bookseller and as such is pleasingly interested in all my writings. Mrs Amery much enjoys the more salacious accounts of my day, which I enjoy relating (I am rather a good mimic and can employ several voices), although I can see it makes Miss Reeve, their other lodger, somewhat nervous.

The other evening I was engaged in telling them a tale from an earlier time concerning the cook Eliza Fanning and the strange case of the poisoned dumplings. Frances, our maid, was just setting down the supper, and I heard her tut-tutting in my ear. I subsequently noticed that Miss Reeve ate nothing, but simply pushed the food round the plate with her fork.

Now, while it was probably not the best choice of story for the dinner table, this was not the actual reason for the lack of appetite. The real problem is that Mrs Amery cannot cook. Some evenings I could beg her for a phial of arsenic.

It is not her fault. She has no feel for food. I have seen her disappear downstairs clutching her copy of *Mrs Beeton's Book of Household Management* (first edition, 1861, marked down to 2 shillings), but whether the end result is veal or venison it would be hard to decipher. Her puddings have us all silenced. They are produced with a triumph that is not warranted. We do all try to make encouraging remarks, but it cannot go on. We are, after all, paying extra for the board, and the board is woeful. Even breakfast is a now a meal that cannot be endured, and I find myself making excuses and dashing off for an early start. Mrs Amery blames everything on the vagaries of the range. If I were to stand up in court on behalf of the prosecution, I would scarcely need to waste time addressing the jury. I would just produce the rabbit in white sauce and ask them to hazard a guess as to what it was, and to decide if the charge of attempted poisoning had been proven. Without bothering to retire, they would to a man shout 'guilty'. We would all be spared our nightly purgatory, and the food would be put out of its misery.

Mr Amery doesn't seem to notice. He is too busy discussing his new mail order book business with his brother-in-law, Mr Hartley. Mr Hartley listens to not a word he is saying, and chatters over the top of him about his day in the hosiery trade, and whether his new novelty stockings should be made in stripes or checks, and does he think socks to match would increase sales? Mr Amery nods sagely and replies, 'Now, books, what do you think of an offer of two for one?' Mr Hartley says, 'Oh, no, they always come in pairs.'

And so it goes on. It certainly makes for a lively supper. The only person who is quite silent is Miss Reeve, who glances at me shyly and smiles every now and again.

Now, here is the rub. I am rather good in the kitchen. At home in Ireland I was always downstairs with Cook, learning the tricks of the trade. I found it utterly absorbing. As a young man, I had no desire to hunt or attend the parties upstairs, I wanted to be downstairs learning how to fold the perfect soufflé, or measure the gelatine for pies and jellies. Cook encouraged me: 'Now, Master Moore, come here and help me knead the barmbrack. You have the special touch.' So it is that potato farls, soda bread and boxty hold no fear for me. My pater had no idea that, when he presumed I was upstairs reading improving works on the law, in reality I was consuming recipes on *haute cuisine*, salivating over decadent sauces and using my knowledge of Latin to discover how Apicius blended 'coriandrum, minutatim succides, teres piper et cuminum' to create the perfect stew.

In Note 15, sub-clause (e) in my 'Rules for Lodgers' (kindly slipped under the door by Mrs A. on my first night), there is particularly mention of the kitchen being 'out of bounds to those who are not family members. The exception to this are the maids who are expected to be handy at all times. The aforesaid maids are not at the behest of the lodger, unless by prior arrangement with the owners or with the owners' representative.'

I have considered this, and have come to the conclusion that, as I am paying for board, I have the right to eat a meal that is fit for consumption. I would also question the use of the plural, I have only seen one maid. The cat is eating better than me, as the mice are fat and are at the moment free-range, wandering round the house as they please. The cat (Arthur) is still finding his feet. Apparently Mr Amery found him wandering near the cemetery looking decidedly lean. I remarked that a cat that can't find meat in a cemetery is not a good candidate for mousing.

Anyway, I am planning to rise early tomorrow, and access the kitchen before Mrs A. comes downstairs.

HANNAH AMERY

Well! I came down this morning, thinking I would ring the changes with maybe a side of fried mushrooms, and who should I find, wearing *my* apron, but Mr Moore! I was speechless. As a barrister, surely he has read and must recollect Note 15, sub-clause (e)? I stayed silent and took the time to look about and absorb the scene. I usually cannot see the range, which, rather like Mr Amery, has a habit of smoking. This morning it was clearly in view, several of my copper pans bubbling and simmering, tamed and brought to heel.

Mr Moore beamed a 'good morning', and said, 'I do hope dear Mrs Amery that you do not think I am flaunting the rules' (which he was), 'but I took a fancy for some eggs Benedict and did not want to put you out.' Eggs Benedict! A smell of warm bread emanated from the range.

On enquiring it turns out that Mr Moore enjoys soda bread in the morning. Had I ever tried it? He took it from the oven and cut me a slice from one end of the loaf. Well, really, I hardly knew what to say, except to enquire after Frances, who it turned out was upstairs laying the fire and preparing the table. He had a small jug of hot chocolate heated and ready on the side. I felt as if I had died and woken up in Brown's hotel, where Mr Amery took me once for tea in headier times. It turns out that Mr Moore's favourite pastime is 'creating' in the kitchen. Would it seem very improper if he offered to cook our supper this evening, really just to indulge his whims? Gaining speech once more, I thought it prudent to say I would be only too happy to indulge him – just this once. Should I send Frances for anything special? He said he would compose a list after breakfast, and if anything did not meet with my wishes or accounts he would suggest a substitute. In the meantime could he continue to be bold and ask us to drop the formal use of his surname. The chaps at school used to call him 'Hilda', and it would be a courtesy to him if we felt we could do the same – also, could I point to where I kept the butter curlers? I hadn't the heart to say we did not to my knowledge own any, so I made a show of rummaging around in the drawer of the kitchen dresser. Mr Moore (now Hilda) said not to worry he would 'make do' and started to fashion a small swan out of our butter with the use of a teaspoon. I said weakly I would be upstairs if needed, and went to find Mr Amery to discuss the new and somewhat unusual developments.

ADA REEVE
Aged twenty-four years, private means

I not one of those girls that men fall for. I don't say this in any way to elicit sympathy, for I am not plain either, just let me say I would not be the first girl chosen for a whirl around the dance floor. My mother used to say, 'Smile and show your teeth, Ada, they are your little pearls in an otherwise rather dull sea.' She did not intend to be unkind – my teeth are a good feature – but it did mean that I have grown up not expecting to be one of those women that can rely on finding a husband. I have a small income, but I am determined to make my own way, and so I have gained the qualifications to become a shorthand typist. I am now up to a rate of 120 words a minute, which I certainly require if only to take down the conversations that occur over supper. Everyone seems to talk at once.

Mr Moore is very entertaining, and has us all gasping over his courtroom dramas. Mr Amery and Mr Hartley talk about their businesses incessantly and how they are going to 'make good'. I have learnt over the years to be a listener, and in order to practise my shorthand skills have taken to noting down some of their ideas. I have also started to amuse myself, when I retire to my room, by making practical suggestions on a ledger sheet of my own design where I analyse the information and put costs against their proposals. I think that Mr Amery may have the seed of a good idea. It may, indeed, be better than even he is aware. He will need to take out more advertisements in order to gain sufficient recognition for the business and I thought his idea of two books for the price of one a good one, but I did not have courage to break into the conversation. Mrs Amery would have him sell fancy goods too. I am not so sure about this, but will work on some figures. I think it would be better to concentrate on the main business before branching out into new lines. It is certainly more interesting than my present work for the Inland Revenue, which is purely copying and the writing of demands.

Mr Hartley needs to think about better designs. I feel that he is playing safe. A lady can take a risk with a pair of stockings in a way she might not with a dress. More colour, more prints. A plain rib is all very well, and I like a black lisle as well as the next, but fashions change and he must adapt or be left behind. I think his use of the word 'novelty' a bad one. It sounds cheap and I for one am not interested in having amusing legs. He should give his stockings names − 'French Fancies', or 'Bicycle Bold' − that would help sales I think. I shall give this some thought.

I am trying to add some of my own touches to the room, so it feels more mine.

I have bought a very pretty paisley cloth, which I have put over the table (I asked Mrs Amery, who, although surprised I wished to cover the wood, was amenable), and have been making a shellwork box to go above the fire. I have been allowed to put up a few pictures that I bought from home (Mr Amery nailing them up for me), so now when I enter it is already starting to feel like . . . well . . . me. My typewriter takes pride of place on the table, as the office has its own. I feel very much in control when I see it. It is my access to a wider world.

Mr Moore has taken over from Mrs Amery in the kitchen. The standard of fare has gone from inedible to delectable. Yesterday evening he came from below with a tower of profiteroles that dripped with chocolate; moored alongside were Jaffa oranges carved into the shape of small boats bobbing about in the sauce. We all clapped. I do not need a mirror to know I am putting on weight.

Mrs Amery calls Mr Moore 'Hilda'– apparently a childhood nickname, but I do not, as it seems presumptuous and I know my mother would not like it.

Mr Moore is very good-looking. I feel quite shy when I glance at him. He seems to do everything well. He not only cooks, but has a way with flowers that is nothing short of professional. He has taken to stopping off at the local barrow on the way home from the courts, and as the weeks progress has become more and more adventurous . Yesterday he came back with long stems of lilies and roses which he combined with fern fronds and a couple of branches of purple leaves he had 'appropriated' from next door's front garden. He handed Mrs Amery a rose from the bunch as he came in: 'Floriography, Mrs Amery. A dark pink rose for "thankfulness".' And then he turned to me: 'And for you, Miss Reeve, a yellow rose for "friendship".' We both blushed, but he did not seem to notice. 'Would you permit me to make use of the china umbrella stand? I have a mind to let these flowers make an entrance.' Mrs Amery just nodded and smiled like the wood doll my father gave me on my tenth birthday, as Mr Moore gathered up his new vase and descended swiftly to the kitchen, eager to get to grips with his floristry. Mrs Amery remarked as he left, 'Miss Reeve, I have a pair of single stem vases, would you care to borrow one? A single bloom always adds a touch of elegance to a room, in a way that cannot always be achieved by a bunch.' I agreed, somewhat surprised at Mrs Amery's tone. I do hope that she is not feeling outshone, it is hard to keep up with such a prodigious talent.

THOMAS HARTLEY
Aged forty-five years, hosiery manufacturer
Brother-in-law to WILLIAM AMERY

I've been manufacturing hosiery for some time now, and I am the first to admit that recently my business has languished. I can trace this back to a year ago when my poor wife, Anne, was taken from me. I have kept the business going, but my heart has not been in it. I have just been going through the motions. It came as a blessing when William suggested I come and lodge with them for a while. I realize now that I have been suffering from loneliness. I didn't recognize the symptoms when I was back home. Anyway, I have rented out my house, and come to live in one room in theirs. It seems a bit topsy-turvy, but I am glad of the change. Nothing could be sadder than walking a house with vacant rooms. William and Hannah are like family, they know when to leave me be and when I need taking out of myself.

Mr Moore and Miss Reeve, my fellow lodgers, are a pleasure to be with, and both in their own way highly unusual. Miss Reeve is a typewriter girl and determined to make her way in the world. She has learnt to master the machine and also to write in shorthand. The other evening she appeared at dinner with a small notebook and pencil. 'Would we mind if she practised her shorthand by taking down some of our conversation? It would help her enormously to build up speeds.' Of course we did not, and to watch her filling the pages with the strange hieroglyphics is an entertainment on its own.

I am thinking of starting a novelty range, I was looking at a young lady on a safety bicycle the other day, and could see that a specialist hose might be a good seller. I was discussing this with William while Miss Reeve scribbled away like a woman possessed.

Talking of hieroglyphics, it was the ancient Egyptians that started the sock trade. An archeologist recently found a matching pair of split-toe red socks while excavating near the Nile. In the illustration they seemed more suited to camels or ducks than people. I may take a visit to go and look at them, as they are on display in the South Kensington Museum. Maybe Hannah would like to accompany me. I do not think she has enjoyed many outings since their enforced move.

I must make mention of tonight's dinner. In my opinion, Mr Moore is wasted in the courts. The main course was cold salmon on a bed of jelly: cucumber strands had been shredded to make seaweed, and the fish scales piped on in a thick mayonnaise. Two vegetable soufflés formed the side dishes, and for pudding we were treated to a marzipan mermaid posing in a spun-sugar cave. The dinner rolls were a delight, the creamed butter moulded into the shape of cowrie shells. I forget the savoury. I do not need a mirror to know I am putting on weight.

HANNAH AMERY

I am putting on weight, as is Mr Amery. I even noticed my dress rings are becoming harder to push on, can it be that I am getting fat fingers? I am not sure how to discuss this with Hilda. He is so pleased to be allowed to showcase his talents that I have not the heart to say anything. He has even started to teach Frances how to knead bread, and she is turning into quite the little baker. There is no doubt he is a treasure. Our ordinary household has become quite extraordinary under his management. Flowers fill the rooms, and our dinners are the height of gourmet dining. How he does it on the budget is a miracle in itself. I was a bit snippy the other day when he came home. He caught me off guard in the hall, talking to Miss Reeve who had also just come in. I am ashamed of myself. I can only put it down to a certain jealousy, which is ridiculous. I have always been very much the heart of the household. Mr Amery relies on me for his well-being, nothing there has changed. But certain responsibilities have unexpectedly passed on to someone younger and certainly more capable. There I have said it! I am feeling elderly and useless. I must get over it. Thomas has asked me to go with him to look at some old socks displayed at the South Kensington Museum. It is not altogether the tonic I had been looking for, but it is an outing. We shall enjoy tea afterwards — just a cup, no cake.

HILDEBRAND MOORE

I knew something was afoot when I brought in the pigeon pie for breakfast this morning. I was greeted not with the usual applause, but with almost a groan. I am professionally attuned to changes in attitude. It comes with the territory. I also believe in plain speaking, so I asked the table straight out to tell me what was amiss. It appears they are all suffering from a surfeit of food! Mr Amery said he had already taken a tincture of nux vomica with his morning coffee, and Mr Hartley said he swore by hepar sulph, and if anyone would care to try some he had a bottle in his room. Soon they were all joining in with their favourite indigestion cures. I am aghast. While I have been labouring to enliven their palates, they have been mixing potions and emollients to settle their stomachs. Why did they not say something earlier? Apparently they did not want to upset me. Upset me! I am mortified. I promised I would give them a plain boiled fowl for dinner, and a light consommé with a simple splash of sherry to settle them.

—◦◦◦—

Every chef has to understand his clientele. I overestimated mine. They are not used to such rich fare and I must adapt accordingly. We are forgoing dinner entirely tomorrow night, as I am taking us all out for a treat to make up for the excesses. I have suggested an exercise evening. Roland Gardens is home to a covered roller-skating rink. There is a band (led by the organist from St Stephen's, Gloucester Road) and a warm and well-lit ladies' room. Mr Amery demurred, saying he was 'too advanced in years for such an undertaking', but I have promised he can wait for us in the reading room, then he can still be included in the party. The ladies are very excited. Mrs Amery has never rollered before and nor has Mr Hartley. I can see I will have be careful they do not over-exert themselves or before I know it there will be cold compresses and cocaine powders all round.

We all left for the outing in high spirits. I have my own roller skates, but the others were left to hire them from the rink. Everything was going rather well. Mr Amery, on seeing that there were several gentlemen of his own age enjoying the sport, decided that he was not going to be left out and would after all take to the floor, where he proceeded at a leisurely to slow pace, holding on to the barrier rail as through life itself depended on it. Miss Reeve took Mr Hartley's arm and together they made a convincing pair with a good to average speed. Emboldened with their success, Miss Reeve then guided Mr Hartley through the nuances of a waltz as the band struck up a lively medley from *The Pirates of Penzance*. The spectators, feeling they had been silent long enough, obliged by giving voice with the choruses. Mrs Amery was at this point in a highly excitable frame of mind. Having started off the evening gingerly, she unfortunately soon lost all fear. She had long since abandoned my protective arm. I watched her lap Mr Amery for a second time, giving him a cheery wave as she whizzed past. I think it was during the second verse of 'A rollicking band of pirates we' that disaster struck. She had reached the end of the rink going at quite the lick. I could see that she had chosen a somewhat reckless angle in which to engage in cornering. I also noted that she had not taken into account a small child just emerging from the stands, or indeed the father pausing mid-roll to perfect the fit of his offspring's skates. Whether she had added the young man going backwards into the calculations of her stopping speed, I did not wait to ascertain. Foolishly, and putting all thoughts of self aside, I managed with a burst of effort to gain on Mrs Amery, grabbing her by the waist just as she was about to vanish over the handrail into the seats beyond. With a skill that would have struck Webb Ellis as masterly, I deposited her somewhat unceremoniously on the wooden floor. Several onlookers gasped in admiration at my rescue skills. However, in the process of this manoeuvre I landed awkwardly, twisting my ankle as I fell. A group rushed to our aid. Mrs Amery was slightly shocked and very embarrassed at her public humiliation, and Mr Amery sprang into action, removing her swiftly from the floor and into the tea room to sit and recover. Miss Reeve and Mr Hartley managed to lift me to my feet and with the aid of Mr Hartley's walking stick and shoulder I hobbled home. On Mrs Amery's return she appeared to administer cold compresses, cocaine powders and copious apologies. I am now off work. Next time I think of an outing please let it be cerebral, maybe an art gallery or the zoological gardens. No balls, bats, bicycles, and certainly not skates.

ADA REEVE

Poor Mr Moore. It was all turning out to be a surprisingly cheerful evening. I have not roller-skated for several years, but it all came back to me in a moment, and I was much enjoying my turn around the floor with Mr Hartley. I had glanced up earlier and spotted Mrs Amery, just about to 'go solo', and pointed her out to Mr Hartley as she went past us at an impressively fast rate. I recall thinking, 'I do hope she has mastered the art of stopping.' The accident could have been a lot worse. The child, his father and the young man going backwards all walked away (in fact I think I heard Mr Amery offering to treat them to tea).

Anyway, Mr Moore will be fine, he is resting with his foot up and Mrs Amery is driving him mad with her attentions. She is also back for the moment in the kitchen, which could have depressed us all, but guess who has come up trumps? Frances! Her time in the kitchen with the master has paid off, and while I would not say that I would trust her with fine dining, she is a good plain cook, and an excellent baker. Mr Moore should be proud, for he has taught her a fine new skill.

I could see her looking at him for approval as she served up yesterday. He never misses a trick and praised her to the hilt, I have never seen her look so happy. I am sure she cannot read, so is having to cook the recipes from memory, which is some feat.

Mr Moore knocked on my door after dinner. He said he needed a change of scene and would I mind if he sat with me for a while. I was perfectly happy, as I usually take an hour to read or go through my work sheets, and I looked forward to the distraction. He sat by my typewriter, absent-mindedly pushing at the keys, and asked what had prompted me to learn the skill. Then his attention was drawn to my ledger sheets, which I had left out thinking to look at them later. He enquired what I was working on, and when I explained that I had been giving time to Mr Amery's book business and Mr Hartley's hosiery, he was amazed, and begged to be allowed to see my workings. I was quite shy at first — it was, after all, just a pastime — but his enthusiasm was very catching and I found myself laying out the papers on the carpet and getting out my shorthand notebook to run through my thoughts. Soon we were both sitting on the floor, Mr Moore's foot resting on my embroidered head-cushion, swapping ideas at a increasingly lively rate, until I could see he was as fired up over the projects as I was.

He asked for a piece of paper and a pencil, and started to sketch a lady who had fallen from her bicycle. Her legs were right up in the air and you could plainly see she was wearing a pair of buttoned boots with her stockings very much in evidence. The lady was smiling and the line underneath read, 'How else could I guarantee you see my specialist Hartley Hose?' I was quite shocked, and said as much to Mr Moore. 'Exactly,' he replied, triumphantly. 'That is precisely how you are supposed to react.'

It turns out he was inspired by the incident at the rink, when Mrs Amery took a tumble, exposing at the same time her undergarments. Mr Moore thinks we (or rather, Mr Hartley) should run a series of advertisements showing ladies who have fallen over while engaging in various sporting activities – skating, riding, lawn tennis, etcetera. He thinks it will appeal to fashionable women who want to seem to be 'of the time', and it will put the more staid and elderly types into such a lather that they will start to discuss the advertisements, thus putting 'Hartley Hose' at the forefront of the trade.

He thinks my idea of calling the hose by name is a good one. Different names for different sporting activities. We spent the rest of the evening thinking up names. I cannot recall enjoying an evening so much. Mr Moore said he felt the same, and could we repeat the exercise tomorrow, and next time put our thoughts towards Mr Amery's books. We both agree that we will share our ideas with the house, but only when they are completed, and we have covered all the angles. Mr Moore is going to use his time off work, when the light is better, to design some of the advertisements. Who would ever have thought I would be spending an evening alone in my bedroom with a young man discussing legs and stockings! My mother would be appalled. I am thrilled.

HANNAH AMERY

Since the 'incident', Hilda has been taking the week off work to recover. It has also meant that he has been housebound. He has in fact taken to his room. Frances goes up in the morning to tidy and lay the fire, but apart from that intrusion, his door remains firmly closed until dinner. I usually knock a couple of times during the day and pop my head round the corner to see if I can be of service. He is always sitting at the table surrounded by papers. At first I thought he had brought court work home, but then I noticed he seems to be sketching pictures of young ladies, with (there is no other way to put this) their legs in the air! He has also been spending a lot of time in the evenings after supper in Miss Reeve's room. I said to Mr Amery have we cause for concern? Mr Amery was not helpful: 'Leave them be. A man with a twisted ankle is an unlikely candidate for Casanova.' Hmm, I am not so sure, women are a soft touch when it comes to an infirmity. Luckily we have a few books to parcel, which will take my mind off the shenanigans upstairs. Perhaps Thomas's influence on a man so young is not a good one. The men never discuss anything other than books and hose at the table, and it must leave its mark. I will ask Mr Amery.

HILDEBRAND MOORE

I must say, who would have thought that shy, sweet Miss Reeve would be hiding such a talent for business. She has her finger firmly on the pulse of retail, and is not only bursting with ideas and enthusiasm, but has costed all her thoughts into a ledger working out plans for the next two years. I am absolutely thrilled that I have twisted my ankle, or I might never have found out what she was doing. I have seen her scribbling away at dinner, but I took her at face value, thinking she really was working up her shorthand speeds. I, of all people, should know to look further than the obvious and not to believe the first thing I am told.

During the day I have taken to working on the drawings and drafts for Mr Hartley's hose. I have been working on various lines to go along with the sketches – 'I've fallen for my Specialist Hartley Hose' is one; 'I'm head over heels for my Specialist Hartley Hose' another. Simple stuff, but memorable. I would drop the word 'specialist', but Miss Reeve tells me that women like to think their legs are in the hands of an expert.

We are also considering whether a small 'H' embroidered on the ankle would enhance the product – or maybe an appliqué of the relevant sport, to encourage purchasing several pairs? I must say I have never thought so much about a woman's legs! Which brings me to another point. I do not think we have long before we will have to admit what we have been up to. Mrs Amery caught sight of my artwork the other day and I could practically see her brain engage. Miss Reeve is taking the brunt of her displeasure but we are prepared to ride out the storm. Tonight we think Books!

ADA REEVE

Oh dear. Mrs Amery could not even bring herself to look at me over dinner. I can see she thinks I have crossed a line. We will have to tell them what we have been working on. I do hope they are not angry and do not think us impertinent. This would never have happened if Mr Moore had not injured his ankle. Well, too late now, we will just have to hope that they are understanding of our efforts. If I think too much about it I feel quite ill with nerves.

Now, books. Mr Amery has not really made any plans for his book business. He has been selling and sending out a few to his old customers, but has not made any inroads into finding new ones. He has not been promoting his books. In short, he needs to try out some new ideas.

We both think that if you buy a book it would be a real incentive to get a second at a reduced price. Sets too would be a good idea, with matching dust covers that create impact on a shelf. We think (we!!) that giving away a bookmark with each copy sold would be a clever way of advertising Mr Amery's business. And, also, he must have a name. We have come up with 'Prose by Post', which is exactly what it is. Mr Moore is throwing legs aside for the next couple of days to draw books, and we plan to reveal all on Sunday. I *do* hope they are not cross. (Worse still, they could ask us to leave!)

THOMAS HARTLEY

I must confess to a feeling of trepidation when Mr Moore and Miss Reeve asked us to gather together in the dining room after we returned from church on Sunday. I glanced at Hannah, who was nudging William, who had lit up a larger pipe than usual, and looked as if he was settling in for a serious dose of bad news. I personally thought they were going to announce their engagement, and I could see Hannah had considered the same thing, her expression one of smiling displeasure.

I was of two minds whether I thought this would be good or bad news. I am fond of both of them, but I cannot see them sharing the grassy path to connubial bliss. Hannah was seated at the table and William and I just hovered round the back as they bustled in carrying a large ledger book and portfolio. Miss Reeve was very pale, looking as though she might need a seat, but Mr Moore was confidence personified, beaming round the room and thanking us for indulging them.

I can safely say that an hour later when they had finished presenting us with their work, we were all stunned into silence. William had picked up one of the drawings — a bookmark, I think — and I just heard him say, 'Remarkable, remarkable', over and over again. I was of the same thought, as I picked up a picture of a young women who had tripped over on a tennis court. 'It's game, set and match, thanks to my Specialist Hartley

Hose', read the copy underneath. Hannah was looking quite tearful, dabbing at her eyes with a small lace hanky. Miss Reeve had by this time sat down. I asked William to fetch her a small glass of sherry, as she was looked quite faint. 'Are we to go?' I heard her say in her quiet voice. 'Go, go where?' I said, before realizing that she meant leave the house.

HANNAH AMERY

Well, as I said to Mr Amery, I am not usually wrong, but I certainly did not see this coming.

I had absolutely decided when we were called to order on Sunday that the two of them were going to announce an engagement. When they had finished showing us their work, I could have cried. I cannot recall anyone ever having shown such an interest in Mr Amery's books. It seems all those endless conversations have been mulled over and dissected by the two of them, their evenings spent working on ways to improve our lot. Of course I always knew that Miss Reeve was a girl of high standards, Hilda too, but I was overwhelmed with a feeling of relief to find there was a simple explanation to the drawings. At best I thought he had taken to designing saucy scenes for comic postcards, and in my worst imaginings I saw the police coming round. The pictures are daring to say the least. It is quite hard for me to look at them without a blush, especially when I gather that I am credited as the inspiration. (I shall never go back to the rink — in fact it is likely I will avoid that entire street.)

Thomas started to question the costs behind the ideas, and Miss Reeve sprang into action with her ledger, reeling off numbers with the aplomb of an accountant. He then asked if he could take the drawings and the figures to study, there being a great deal to absorb, and it was Sunday. He gathered up the work, and then said, 'I think I speak for all of us, when I say that I am not only touched, but impressed. You have issued us a wake-up call. While we have languished, and indulged ourselves with worthless chit-chat, you have actioned a plan. As we say in the trade, you have "knocked my socks off". The time is right to reinvent the wheel! From now on it's going to be "legs up" for Specialist Hartley Hose. What say you, William?'

WILLIAM AMERY

Never would I have imagined that taking in lodgers would bring about such a change in fortune. I realize now that I viewed the whole experience as a necessary trial, and just hoped at the best they would not be too disruptive. I think it was when a box arrived from the printers filled with the new bookmarks stamped 'Prose by Post', that I felt at last I had someone on my side. Books can be a lonely trade — not the books themselves you understand, I could look and read until the lamps are too dim to see by — but there is rarely an opportunity to discuss the business side of the operation. Of course I have Mrs Amery, but that is not the same as having someone who is completely independent glance at the facts and figures.

I decided (along with Mrs Amery) that we had nothing to lose by adopting wholesale, so to speak, their ideas. I made appointments with the publishers and, armed with the figures provided by Miss Reeve and the drawings from Hildebrand (I am sorry, I find that 'Hilda' does not trip off the tongue), we have persuaded them to drop their margins while we trial the 'two for one' concept. We also secured permission to use matching dust jackets so we have a collection of titles that will make up highly attractive gift sets. Mrs Amery has agreed to postpone the pleasures of the bath. It should have arrived months ago, but Crappers have taken so many orders that there is a delay in the deliveries. Lucky for us as the bath funds can now be redirected towards newspaper advertisements. Hildebrand and Miss Reeve completely concurred, so it is to be business before baths for the time being.

Thomas is equally committed. He came home yesterday with samples of the new stockings.

We were like children, opening the packs and admiring the designs. I had a bottle of Veuve Clicquot that I had kept from our West End heyday, so we toasted to our success and then chinked our glasses and cried 'health to the lodgers', as Hildebrand called downstairs saying to Frances she could 'bring it up now'. Frances appeared carrying a cake formed into a lady's leg, the foot teetering atop a pile of books (Hildebrand informed us it was fruitcake, 'to hold shape'). We had quite the party, which ended in us all singing a round of 'A rollicking band of pirates we' to commemorate Mrs Amery's inspirational crash. Mrs Amery then heard knocking through the wall from next door, which signalled an end to our celebrations. I feel ten years younger.

GOING DOWN, GOING DOWN

It was only a matter of time before 'Prose by Post' outgrew the small front parlour. Books are neither the lightest nor the smallest of goods, and soon the room was overrun with boxes. Evidently a more suitable dispatch area would need to be found, and Thomas Hartley came up trumps. By clearing a large back room in his factory, he made a working space for the Amerys' book business. This made sense, as they agreed to share the costs of the dispatch and warehouse staff, which benefited all. This cosy arrangement was soon extended when the three made the decision to move back into Thomas's house. Some of the capital from Finborough Road was used to grow the businesses, and family life returned to fill the rooms in Thomas's old home once more.

Hildebrand Moore abandoned the law, and Ada Reeve gave in her notice to the Inland Revenue. Their agency 'Moore and Reeve' set up offices near Bond Street where they specialized in marketing and the placement and design of advertisements. They became renowned for their use of distinctive fonts and rather sensational artwork. The agency continued to advise Mr Amery and Mr Hartley and the five remained close friends as their fortunes continued to grow.

Frances Holt went from maid-of-all-work to become cook at no. 73, a meteoric rise entirely due to her tutelage under Mr Moore.

Sadly, the roller rink closed down to make way for further housing, but leisure activities in the vicinity boomed as Earl's Court Exhibition site continued to extend, much boosted by the success of Buffalo Bill's 'Wild West', which attracted over fifteen thousand people to the area over a five-month season. Soon other earthly delights to be found in Earl's Court included a switchback railway and a water-toboggan slide, and the whole area could be observed from a bird's-eye view sitting aloft on the 'The Great Wheel', which dominated the local skyline. This was also the start of the bicycle boom and a local ladies' cycling club, 'The Wheel', was established in Bolton Gardens.

———◦◦◦———

For a brief period William Holier, and his wife, Sarah, have the key to no. 53. William was born in Newbold-on-Stour, and his income is derived from 'interest of money and house property'. He sells after two years to a bank clerk, David Robinson, who lives a punctual, trustworthy and discreet life there until his increased salary allows him to marry and move on. Finborough Road continues to decline.

We are now in 1901. Geoffrey Harbird and his wife Ellen have the key to the house. Ellen also has two teenage children from a previous marriage, both in residence. Geoffrey has a small private income, but not nearly enough to support the family. He needs lodgers. He rents to Annie Walsh, a dressmaker, and her young daughter Olive, a typist. Moira O'Hull and her two sisters also reside there; all work as bodice-makers. He manages to squeeze in Esthanie Newman, seventy-two years old, along with her son, Joseph, and daughter, Kipper. Even at a time when domestic labour is cheap there are no spare funds; the Harbirds cannot even run to a maid-of-all-work. This is the lowest point in the fortunes of the house.

THE NEW KEYHOLDERS

THE ENTERPRISE
SPRING 1901

GEOFFREY HARBIRD
Aged forty-one years, independent means

The first thing I did when I saw the house was to count the rooms. I have enough funds, thanks to a small legacy, to purchase the property, but not enough to actually put food on the table. This is a vital requirement, as I recently acquired a wife. Ellen is not on her own a big eater, but she has brought as part of her dowry two children, who like nothing better than eating – hence the room count. Lodgers are the way forward and I have taken in eight. Four are planning to work from their rooms; they are all in the dressmaking trade. We also have Mrs Newman, an aged widow living on a small inheritance. She too brings a package: a son and a daughter, a pathetic pair, both having reached middle age without a life between them. They rely entirely on their mother, as she does on them. Still, I am not concerned with personal relationships. Cash, no questions. That is a contract everyone understands.

I do not look on this little enterprise as a long-term business. I have an aged aunt who is expected to provide a second windfall. She has no children of her own, and has taken me on as her heir. It is no particular secret that her lungs seem to trouble her. I have noticed of late a slight whistling in her breath when we talk, and while I do not want to appear mercenary, I see no point in expressing a sentimentality I do not feel. In the meantime my stepson John, who is fifteen, has got himself a job as a district post messenger – well, it's a start. Maud, my stepdaughter, is thirteen and helps around the house with light chores, while Ellen attends the rooms and the kitchen. I have more than enough to do worrying about the finances, but I take a break when I can. There is a pub down the road where I might choose to sit for a while with a small glass. It does me good to be out of the house, which does start to feel claustrophobic after a while. Ellen knows where to find me if I am needed, and can send Maud to bring me home.

ELLEN HARBIRD
Aged thirty-nine years
Wife to GEOFFREY

I seem to be in sole charge of running Geoffrey's 'little enterprise'. I am a good worker and I don't think of myself as lazy, but there are four flights and I seem to be always on them. He has rented out all our rooms, and also charges attendance fees, and as I am the attendant, it never stops. I have Maud to help me: she carries the hot water to the rooms, and never complains, no matter how many times they ask.

Geoffrey also charges for meals, which I can and do provide, but it leaves me no time over for anything – and the washing! Luckily, our lodgers are not flush (otherwise, let's be honest, they wouldn't be here), so they are not particularly demanding in this department. Mrs Newman wants clean sheets, and Miss Olive, who works as a typist, likes to be well turned out, but as long as the others have a Sunday blouse they are content. I send some of it out, which annoys Geoffrey, but I have reminded him we are saving on a maid, cook and bottle-washer, and we want to keep the lodgers we do have, so something has to give. He has reluctantly agreed that the sheets can go to Susan, who collects. Geoffrey has his own work, although I am somewhat in the dark as to what it is. It is easier for me if he is out of the house, otherwise he adds to my burdens with complaints and instruction.

My first husband died when the children were small, and I think myself fortunate to have Geoffrey provide for us all, but life takes its toll. I used to be so pretty – men have often complimented me on my appearance – now when I look at myself I do not recognize that young girl. There is no time for the niceties of dress and my hair is a fright, and thin . . . oh, for a plump arm!

We have inherited a cat. Unlike me he is rather fat, and he seems to be keeping the mice under control, if not completely at bay. He lives in the kitchen, and Maud is very attached to him, she calls him Mr Fin. He is quite handsome. I was surprised to find him when we arrived. A sensible cat would have left with the previous tenants. He obviously knows something about the neighbourhood I do not, and so chooses to stay. When we arrived I discovered some card bookmarks. I own a Bible and a couple of penny novels, so I kept them, and also gave some out to Mrs Newman and the ladies. Maud has one too, and is very proud of her acquisition; it is hidden in a small wooden box with her other treasures. There was also a rather battered old tray with pasted pictures, and a blue-patterned ginger jar with a chip on the lid. The jar looks attractive on the mantelpiece, and I have turned it round to hide the break. The tray too is in use for carrying dinners up to the lodgers.

I am so proud of John. He has been taken on as a post office telegraph boy. He has a uniform, and they may issue him with a bicycle soon. At the moment he is delivering on foot. He tells me that he averages twelve miles a day. I tell him so do I. He has ambitions to become a clerk. We will see. I say he is already my man of letters. He and Geoffrey don't get on. He says Geoffrey treats me as his slavey, and is more in the pub than home. He is about right. My only ambition now is that Maud does not follow in my footsteps. She no longer attends school, but she can read all the newspaper and has a very neat script. Geoffrey would have sent her out to earn, but I have said I need her here – which, sadly, I do. I have thoughts of her working in a shop, or maybe becoming a typist like Miss Olive.

I tell her, be a woman on your own terms. A husband can bring you down. As an example of this, Geoffrey has proved a good role model.

JOSEPH NEWMAN
Aged thirty-eight years, assistant square-keeper

My father made us promise when he died to look after mother, and so we have. She is a good woman. She sounds off, but means nothing by it, she would give us the world if she could. Mr Harbird, who owns this establishment, has taken to making sneering asides when he sees me. 'Milksop, mother's boy', that sort of thing. Why? I do him no harm. I make no reaction, which clearly irritates him more. Thankfully he is out a lot, and it is his wife who looks after us. Mother pays over the rent each week. He turns up for that, counting it before he leaves the room, as though she might cheat him of a shilling.

I have worked, of course, but each time I start I am called back to mother, who is sick and needs me. Employers do not like a man who is not reliable. In fact I have recently been taken on part-time helping the square-keeper in Redcliffe. I enjoy it as much as any of my other jobs. Being outside suits me. I am really a glorified path-sweeper.

Mrs Harbird never stops. Maud, her daughter, is a worker too, up and down with trays of food and water. I helped her carry one the other day, but she followed me up protesting all the way; such was her vehemence it would have been simpler to let her proceed with the task.

Mrs Harbird was sweeping the steps as I went out this morning. She looked up and I suddenly noticed she has the prettiest grey eyes. I greeted her as I went past and she smiled. Her features transformed from drudge to beauty in that second. How is it that the worst of men seem to attract charming women? My sister, Kipper, nearly married a complete waster. It was a piece of luck when he threw his lot in with another, but she still talks of him. Mother says, 'Good riddance. I never liked him.' Which is not in the circumstances helpful.

JOHN TAYLOR
Aged fifteen years, district post messenger
Son to ELLEN HARBIRD,
Stepson to GEOFFREY HARBIRD

We met him by the Great Wheel. Yellow waistcoat, teeth and a smile. Ma had taken us there for a look and a walk round. He came and stood by us. Asked if we would like a ride. I said we were all right. He asked if Father was here. No. 'Go on, have a ride. It's on me.' Maud all excited and nodding at Ma. How kind. Smiler and Ma in the front seats, Maud and me behind. Up to the top and down to the bottom. Dizzy heights. His arm round her shoulders as they start to go down.

We were living with my aunt, Ma's sister. Smiler starts to call. First it's a walk to the bandstand, the following week tea at the A.B.C. How kind. The Clapham Grand and Dan Leno, that was the nail in our coffin. Engaged. Married six weeks later, and her with two children. How kind.

He had some money from a windfall, and put it all into a house on the Finborough Road. He's doesn't do carrying. Pay servants, not likely. Ma can do the work. Lucky to have him. So kind. He calls it his 'little enterprise'.

I really am the lucky one, I have got myself a job with the post office, and a uniform. It is a job with prospects. If I work hard, I could be a clerk there one day. Mr Harbird (very formal, very polite, I can see it annoys him) takes my wages each week. He leaves me a couple of shillings. I am staying put for Ma. He would not hit her, that's not his style. How kind. He's more of a wear-you-down type of a man. Sneer, then expect you to be grateful. He is out a lot. Suits me. I will be sixteen in a couple of months. I am getting fitter on the job, growing taller too. I will soon be able to show him unkind.

JOSEPH NEWMAN

I was on my way to Redcliffe Square, only gone a couple of blocks, when who should I see?

Mr Fin. He was purring his way round the legs of a young woman and followed her down into the basement. I heard her calling him 'Arthur'. So Mr Fin is leading a double life. I will have to tell Maud. On second thoughts, I know she is very fond of the cat, and I would not want to upset her. I will mention it to Mrs Harbird. Now I know why he is so round. He would be out of a job if he was my mouser. He lacks the killer instinct. A bit like me. I understand Mr Fin, I too am more of a sit, watch and don't bother me sort. I am now edging the paths in the square and planting out spring bulbs around the borders. I asked if I can take a couple. I plan to pot them up for Mrs Harbird. I would like to see that smile again.

ELLEN HARBIRD

While the cat's away . . . isn't that how the rhyme goes? Here's me thinking Mr Fin was eating at home, when all the time he was getting his tea from no. 73. He has been absent for two nights, so on information from Mr Newman I went up the road to search for him. I knocked on the basement door, which was answered by a young woman, clearly the cook, and there sitting on a chair was Mr Fin. I have the whole story. He went missing from our house on the day of the move, and recently reappeared at the back door of 73. His name is Arthur. The cook is called Frances, and she used to work in our house. She is clearly a very good cook. There was a pile of golden buns on the table and a chicken bubbling in a broth that made my mouth water to smell it. I explained how my daughter has adopted Mr Fin (now Mr Arthur Fin), and her heart would break to lose him. Frances says that I may take Mr Fin back, and that if he returns to her (and, really, why wouldn't he?), Maud is welcome to come and visit. Her family are very obliging, and keen for her to stay put, so will not object. The previous cook drank with a lively enthusiasm and the one before that was in the family way before the soup had gone tepid on the table.

She is funny. I am glad to have found a friend. Not that I have time for friends – the enterprise is all-consuming – but at least someone to greet if I pass them on the street. Frances gave me a bag of the buns to take home, and said to send Maud down so she could see where Mr Fin had been staying and to rest assured he was in good hands. I returned home in quite a cheerful state, which continued when Mr Newman came down to the kitchen, first to enquire about the cat, and then to present me with a little pot of earth. He says there are bulbs living under the soil, which will grow if I keep them watered and in the light. How kind. I smiled.

ESTHANIE NEWMAN
Aged seventy-two years, widow of independent means
Mother to JOSEPH

I know his sort. He thinks that because I am old and in reduced circumstances I am stupid too. Puts on a loud voice when he comes to get the rent, when one thing I am not is deaf. He used to try the odd pleasantry, telling me it was a 'nice day' or 'looking lovely, as usual'. He soon stopped that when he noticed I wasn't going to be flannelled by chit-chat. Now he just pushes his way in, and takes the money which I have ready on the table for him. He is rude to Joseph whenever he sees him, which makes me seethe. More of a gentleman you would never find than Joseph. He would have done all right if it hadn't been for me. I had hoped to be able to leave him something when I go, but in the end I am afraid all he will have is my diamond engagement ring and a small locket that his father gave me when we met. He may be looking after Kipper too, unless she finds herself a widower, which she won't do if we stay on in this house.

I would look for other accommodation, but the rooms we have are a good size, which is important as Kipper and I must share.

Mrs Harbird is a pleasant and helpful woman. She came up when we arrived with a little bookmark as a gift for me, and only today appeared with a delicious bun she thought I might enjoy. Harbird himself is mostly out, so causes us no real bother apart from the Friday confrontation.

It is strange how life turns out. You start off with hope and expectations, and seem to be on the high road, and then an unexpected twist sends you off on a spiral. I have been plagued all my life with ill health — not helped, I suspect, by the black fogs of London — but I am strong in spirit. In fact, I refuse to be brought down.

I'll say now I have no time for a bully. The skilful kind that can sweet-talk a woman. The kind that offer love by feigning interest, feigning support, feigning kindness. As soon as she succumbs to this flattery that's when he can start his real game. It might begin with a joke, just 'a bit of a laugh'. Maybe she has a walk he can copy, or something in her speech. Then he will move on to exclude her friends and family — so much better when it's 'just the two of us'. Soon every activity she engages in is deemed unsatisfactory, and friends have become a thing of the past. She has become a piece on his board to be moved or discarded, built up and brought down. Sadly, too, a willing player, who sees only the good in him and the faults in herself.

The man who wanted to marry Kipper was like that. She was so full of life, yet I could see the happiness being crushed from her every time they met. I thanked God when he moved on to a new woman, leaving me to pick up her pieces. The fact she still talks about him sends me wild.

'Good riddance,' I said, when he left. This Harbird's the same — bad rubbish. I can smell him coming up the stairs.

GEOFFREY HARBIRD

There is something about old women I cannot stand. Always have a look as if they know better than you. The one upstairs is just like that. Looks straight into my eyes when I collect the money. It gives me the creeps. I tried to be polite, pass the time of day, but she wasn't having any of it.

This is my house and I will say who does or doesn't stay in it. One word from her and it's 'out the door the lot of you'. Ellen is too nice to them. I caught her smiling at the son the other afternoon when I came home. 'Save your smiles for me,' I said. 'The one who puts food on the table.'

Ask any of my friends, I am a personable fellow. Buy anyone a drink, pass the time of day. If they had to sum me up in a word I think it would be 'kind'. I won't be taken for a ride though, I'm not a soft touch. Some thought I was mad to marry a woman with a couple of children, when I could have my pick. I said, 'She's a steady sort. Good around the house.' And of course there's nothing wrong with a bit of gratitude. Thankful, that's Ellen. It takes a certain sort of man to take on another's children. I like it when she smiles at me.

After all, I deserve it.

ANNIE WALSH
Aged thirty-eight years, widow and dressmaker

I love a bit of froth. Lace and ribbons are like an opiate to me. There is nothing that can't be cured by looking at a roll of organza ribbon. I should have been born to money. I would have delighted in fashions. There are not many that can find a sleeve as fascinating as I do. I never tire of working out a pattern for tape lace, or draping a lawn dress until the train hangs just so. I keep a box of remnants. A scrap of green velvet, a triangle of tweed, a piece of lacework — every fragment reminds me of my work, and I see before me a vision of the woman wearing it. I make mental pictures of her entering a room, throwing off a mantle or standing by a fireplace, a lace collar brightening her features. I see them as brilliant creatures, made lovelier through my skills.

I do a lot of work for a young lady, Mrs Sullivan, in the Boltons. Every spring she goes on her pilgrimage to Paris, and brings back wonderful fabrics and extraordinary trimmings. I copy the clothes she has bought from the various studios, and I pour over copies of *Les Modes*, so I can add touches of my own. You would never think what I create from my little room. I stitch every hour I can by the gas until my fingers start to protest, or on occasion refuse to straighten. The pay is pitiful, but how else would I get my hands on fabric that has crossed an ocean? The girls upstairs are on piecework. Making bodices for the couturiers on Burlington Street. I couldn't. I need to see the completed outfit, I need to see that picture.

I have made Olive, my daughter, a little tailored suit for work. The skirt just clears the floor and the blouse is simple but with a trimmed cuff. Topped off with a beret, she looks like a fashion plate when she leaves for work.

She is a secretary, works for an author in Chelsea, typing up his manuscripts.

I am not particularly bold but children make you step up, and the thought of Olive in service sent a shiver through me. One afternoon I was at The Boltons, Mrs Sullivan was about to have a fitting for a particularly beautiful evening skirt (Brussels lace, silk satin, bugle beading). As I was entering my ears picked up the tap-tapping of a typewriter. While Mrs Sullivan twirled and preened, I heard a voice ask if she had a secretary. She looked at me rather vaguely and nodded. I was adjusting the hem when I heard the voice again, 'How I wish my Olive could gain such a skill.' Mrs Sullivan looked down at the top of my head and answered, 'Really? So why doesn't she?'

Sounds limped out. No machine, lessons too expensive. There was a period of silence while I pinned up a ruffle and she gave a twirl, then, 'Let her come here. I am out mid-mornings. My secretary will give her an hour's instruction and she may use our machine. That will do for now. Please return the skirt as soon as you have completed the hem. And I think a few more beads around the panels would be pretty.'

I was the colour of a beetroot. I thanked her, nodding like a madwoman, scooped up the skirt and left. So that was how Olive received her lessons, and why she is a typist. We are saving up for a course in shorthand, then Olive can get a better position.

I would like to say that Mrs Sullivan had given thought to her offer. That she has a charitable disposition, or a desire to forward the conditions of a working girl, but the truth is she likes to appear to her friends as a forward-thinking woman. The lessons did not affect her one way or the other — I doubt she ever knew when or if Olive was in the house.

But I appear churlish, when of course I am very grateful. Her secretary was a pleasant women and pleased for a break from the daily work, to instruct a young and willing pupil.

I noted Mrs Harbird's daughter on the stairs yesterday. She is a sweet girl. Maybe Olive can help her to a trade. The time is coming for us women to stick together, and Mrs Harbird looks as if she could do with a hand. I have a length of cotton spare; if I have the time I shall make Maud a dress. They should give out clothes instead of pills, nothing improves health and well-being like a new outfit. I think depression would be a thing of the past if everyone had their pick of beautiful clothes.

ELLEN HARBIRD

I had a funny dream last night. The stairs had been replaced with wooden boards, and while I had slid effortlessly from the top of the house into the kitchen, I could not claw my way back up to the top, I would manage a few feet and then slip backwards, ending up by the sink. That's it, I am losing my mind over the staircase.

I know every crack and creak of this place. I have not managed to get back to see Frances since Mr Fin disappeared. Maud is often down there, and enjoys talking to her and Mr Fin. I don't let Geoffrey know, or he would find outside work for her.

Our lodgers are a good bunch. The girls work the hours that I do, stitching and sewing. I often hear them laughing together. Mrs Walsh is a happy soul too. Whenever I see her she calls me in to look at a fashion plate in a magazine and ask what I think of the outfits. I find it hard to take an interest. I think I am too tired. Mrs Walsh has made Maud a dress. It is much too lovely for her to wear every day. Indeed I have hidden it away so Geoffrey does not find it. I know it would annoy him, I can hear him now, a lecture on 'nosy' people. He would have given the dress back. I told Mrs Walsh I was keeping it 'for best'. I am still thinking how to get Maud a proper job. Mrs Walsh asked if I would come up and sit with her one day for half an hour, so we could get acquainted. I said I would like that very much, which is true. I can think of nothing I would rather do (other than sit in the kitchen at no. 73 with Frances and Maud). In fact I am going to do it! Friday would be good, when Geoffrey has taken the rents and retired to the Finborough.

—◦◦◦—

Half an hour with Annie was like a tonic. I don't really talk to people, other than to take instruction. She certainly loves dresses. She showed me her remnant box. Filled with the prettiest scraps. I rubbed a piece of cream silk velvet against my cheek – it was the softest thing I have ever touched. As she talked about her ladies I felt quite tearful. I had no idea that an outfit could move you so. She had pulled a piece of chiffon from a trunk, and placed it round my shoulders, and then put her glass before me. She was quite triumphant as she saw me well up. 'They do that,' she said. 'Clothes change you.'

I found I just talked about myself, which is something I never do. Annie enquired how I had met Geoffrey, and I told her about the A.B.C and Dan Leno and how he used to be so kind, and he had expectations of a windfall. I said too much. It was like I had turned on the kitchen tap and it wouldn't stop flowing. 'Comedy and cake are a heady mix. Remember to find time for yourself, Ellen,' she said as I went. 'You deserve it.'

As I went downstairs I felt in my pocket and there was the little piece of velvet. It is a reminder of all the things in my life that are missing. My fingers clutched at it like a charm. I shall keep it, and wish for better times. As I got to the kitchen I looked at my pot and noticed a small green spike pushing up through the earth. I smiled.

JOHN TAYLOR

The last few days returning from my rounds I have noticed a woman standing and looking up at our house. She doesn't stop long. I can't think what she sees to look at. I have stood on her spot a couple of times and looked up, but nothing catches my eye. Anyway, she hasn't been by today. Maybe she has heard we have lodgings and is looking for somewhere to stay. I expect Geoffrey (I have taken to calling him Geoffrey in a pally way, which confuses and irritates him more than a formal approach) will find a spot for her by the range, or maybe she can tuck in under the stairs. The enterprise needs a few more bodies to trip over.

I am pleased Maud has found a friend up the road. I noticed she has been putting on weight, as she has taken to having dinner while she is down there. I wish Ma could go there too, but she daren't risk Geoffrey turning up and finding her out. Ma has been happier of late. She seems to have made a friend of Mrs Walsh, and Mr Newman is nice too. I winked at Miss Olive as she went by the other day. She pretended not to see. There is something about a uniform that gives a man standing. I might ask where she works, I think it is near by. I could meet her and walk her back. Some of the other messengers have a girl, so I think I should too. Ma laughed when I told her. She thinks I should be out playing with the lads. I am sixteen now. A respectable wage-earner. I sometimes get a tip when I deliver the telegrams, I am putting the money by, hidden in a blue china jar on the mantel. He won't look in there.

GEOFFREY HARBIRD

Oh dear, oh dear. Young John was in a sulk today. I found some money in an old jar on the mantelpiece. I thought that Ellen had been keeping it from me, but it turns out it is John who is the little squirrel. I said, you will have to try harder than that, my son (I can see the word annoys him). Remember, we are all the same family now. Share and share alike. You can't expect a roof and food for free. That wouldn't be right, would it? Well if looks could kill . . . he clenched a fist. I thought, here's a thing – he's going to take a swing. But then I thought, hang on, he won't want that smart uniform to get ruined. It's hard to hit a man when you've a little peak cap on. I was right. He just flushed up, turned heel and left the house.

Ellen came up from the kitchen to see what the noise was. She said 'That's the lad's money. He's saving up.' Saving for what? His own bicycle? Ellen said I push him too hard. If I'd kept money from my dad he'd've chucked me out the house there and then, with a boot up the arse for good luck. John has it soft, like his mother.

Anyway, I took the coins and went back to the Finborough. I told Ellen I'd thought of taking her down there for a bit of an outing but, as I pointed out, the men go for a break not a funeral. I said, 'A few more smiles from you, and we could have a fine time. Try to tidy yourself up a bit. You were pretty when we first met.'

I think it's important to keep a woman up to the mark, otherwise they forget themselves.

JOHN TAYLOR

He has taken my money.

I wanted to hit him, but Ma has always told me fists are a last resort. I walked away. I am not sure her advice is the best. I would have felt much better if he had been laid flat on the ground with blood gushing out of his ears.

I saw that woman again today. What is she up to? I am going to wait tomorrow and speak to her.

I talked to Miss Olive today – nothing exciting. Asked where she worked. I should have done better. It is tricky to have a chat in the hall. I saw that Mr Newman gave ma a flower pot, she was really pleased. Perhaps I should find Miss Olive a gift, but now all my money has gone. I would rather we had starved than come to live in the enterprise. That's not quite right though. I have met Miss Olive and Mr Newman. It's not the enterprise, it's Geoffrey. He will have to go. Death by an omnibus would be too good for him. I shall spend the day thinking up ways to shift him. It will make the deliveries go faster.

JOSEPH NEWMAN

I have a problem. I have noticed on my way to work a woman looking up at the house. She looks a respectable sort, never stays long. I thought at first she was searching for lodgings, but then I realized she never thinks to come up or down the steps, let alone knock. I have surmised she is maybe waiting for someone.

I approached her yesterday, but just as I was about to greet her she scuttled off. It is a bit of a mystery. I do not want to alarm Mrs Harbird, who has been quite smiley of late, and has made a friend of Annie Walsh, but I think she should know if someone is watching her home.

John has taken a shine to Miss Olive. I heard him the other morning as they were both leaving for work trying to make a conversation. I felt for him – in fact I would have liked to help him out. You would think that getting older would make those sort of overtures easier, but I have not found it so.

Luckily I am a good listener, and really do prefer the stories of others' lives to my own – in fact I find them a source of endless interest, the whys and the wherefores. You would think my mother, having led a very closeted life, would have little insight into human behaviour, but she can sum a person up with a glance. I think I must have inherited a bit of that. When John comes home tonight I will try to give him a word of encouragement. Maybe we can take a walk around the block. Easier to talk if we aren't in the enterprise.

Well, as it turned out the talk was of interest. We went to Redcliffe Square, and I showed him my work, and how the bulbs were coming up, and told him there might even be a full-time job coming my way, as the head gardener was pleased with my efforts. Anyway, one thing led to another, and he asked me if I had seen this woman looking at our house – which, of course, I had. We started to converse over what she might be seeking. We agreed that she was clearly nervous, and certainly taking her time about whatever concerned her. John said did I think she was Geoffrey's fancy woman? I didn't. He looked quite downcast at that.

Sister? Relation? If so, why doesn't she just knock ? Maybe it's not Geoffrey but someone else in the house she's looking for –

but who? We have agreed that as the older party I am to be the one to speak to her. As she is not keen to engage in conversation I will have to be a bit lively to catch her, but catch her I will.

We talked about Miss Olive too. I told him to wait outside the house for her to leave. Much easier there than in the hall for all to hear. I said, just ask her if she would like a walk with you next Sunday afternoon. Chances are she will be pleased to have a young man escort her round the Boltons. I said I would lend him the money for a cup of tea, so he could treat her. Think of her as your friend, I said, not your girl. Just enjoy the company and see where it takes you. He seemed quite buoyed up as we went back, and thanked me as we went in. Mrs Harbird came up the stairs, took off John's cap and ruffled his hair, which I could see irritated him. Mothers just can't let you be.

Well nothing goes quite according to plan. For the next couple of days the lady did not appear. In fact I began to think that whatever had drawn her to the street had resolved itself. I was just leaving no. 53 on the third day, accompanied by Mrs Walsh, who was making a delivery of blouses, when I spotted her coming up the road towards the house. Without saying anything to Mrs Walsh I swiftly left her side and walked towards the woman. As I passed her I grabbed on to her wrist, causing her to cry out. Mrs Walsh came running up, saying what was I doing? Had I lost my senses? All the while the woman writhed and twisted to get away from my grasp. The next thing I knew Frances the cook and cat-stealer was at my side, demanding pretty much the same thing. I held on, talking over the top of the woman's hat, trying to explain to the others what I was about. Frances took control. She held the lady by the other arm and marched us all off to the basement kitchen of no. 73. She then tipped Mr Fin off his chair on to the floor and pushed the stranger into it. Mrs Walsh stayed standing by the door, blouses at the ready, in case the women tried to make a run for it. I begged for calm, as everyone was talking at once, trying to ascertain what was what. The story which came out first in drips and then a positive torrent was an extraordinary one, and took some telling and absorbing.

The lady's name was Christine Harbird, née Baxter, married for the past six years to one Geoffrey Harbird, and mother of his two children. She lives with the children in Camden Town. About eighteen months ago Geoffrey left the house on the pretext of meeting a man. He had not been seen since. Mrs Harbird had in fact at the time informed the police, who after making rudimentary enquiries lost interest. She has carried on as best she could, but found it hard to get on with life, always wondering if he was around the next corner.

Well, the three of us were struck dumb. Frances rustled her up a cup of tea and some biscuits, which seemed to relieve the lady (indeed, she paused in her tale to enquire how Frances had 'got them so short?').

Apparently, six weeks ago, she had taken the children for a treat to the Earl's Court exhibition.

There, in the distance, wearing the same yellow waistcoat he had walked out in, was Geoffrey.

He soon disappeared from view. Hampered by the crowd and her children, Mrs Harbird (the first) could not follow him. Knowing that Geoffrey had an interest in pubs, she began going round the local establishments. For days she had no luck, until she came upon the Finborough. After describing her man to the landlord it transpired to be nothing short of a miracle that Geoffrey was not ensconced at the bar, or at his regular table by the window.

It was mentioned that he ran a little enterprise of lodgers from no. 53, and his wife should be able to help with any enquiries. Mrs H. (the first) did not understand the reference to a wife, but was reluctant to confront Geoffrey in a pub full of strangers, so she had decided to wait by the front door to catch him as he left the house. This had not been successful. She did not seem to grasp the notion that he had married again. She just kept saying, rather crossly, 'But he is married to *me*.' It was soon clear that, although she thought Geoffrey was far from an ideal mate, she also thought it only fair that the one who had married him first was the one who should claim any little windfall that he might have. I couldn't help thinking this was correct.

Well, we all needed time to absorb the tale. Who should tell Ellen? Geoffrey had clearly fallen foul not only of his wives but also the law. I said to Mrs H., 'Please give us a couple of days. The lady who thinks she is the official Mrs Harbird has done no wrong, and we have to think out the best course of action.' Amazingly, this was agreed on. She gave us her address in Camden Town, shook our hands, apologized to Frances for taking up her kitchen (and please could she have the biscuit recipe?), and left, saying she would look forward to hearing from us as soon as. She had a mind to inform the police, but a few days would make little difference.

We all stood looking at one another. Until Frances said 'Cup of tea, anyone?', and we all nodded. I felt a bit sick. I could only think of the distress this information was going to cause Ellen. I could see the other two felt the same. We also realized that it would mean leaving no. 53. Annie said, 'I need to deliver these blouses or I won't get paid.' And I had to get to the square or the same went for me. We agreed to meet back in the kitchen later that day. I needed the air.

GEOFFREY HARBIRD

Women. Can't they take a hint? You would have thought that just the fact of leaving the house and not coming back would cause the penny to drop. I'd stuck with Christine for six years. Long years they were, too. Nag, nag, nag. Always going on about something. I thought I was doing her a favour. I used to say to her, keep going on and I'm out of here. Then on the day I received my little windfall I thought bugger it. Start again. Find a woman who's a bit more appreciative, more amenable. I thought, don't upset her with a row, just nip off and out. I told nobody where I was, except the aunt, who never liked Christine anyway. Well, obviously I didn't tell her everything. I like to keep a few secrets. Just that Christine was a flirt and a nag, and I needed a break, and to keep it to herself if anyone came looking. Which they did and she has.

I hadn't really planned to remarry, but then there was Ellen, smiley and grateful, and I thought why not make the girl happy? No skin off my nose. Just say a few words, and we can all live in harmony. Who could believe that Christine would track me down? So like a woman, they can't just move on, have to have the final say.

Well what to do now? Luckily the landlord at the Finborough mentioned a woman was on the look-out for me, and I'm guessing all hell will be breaking loose at no. 53. Toes lively, I think. I have a mate over by Twickenham and I can lay low with him, while I consider the options. Money is what will calm Christine. Make her an offer, that is the way. Cash, no questions.

In fact, forget Twickenham. I will go over to Camden and see how the land lies. The children will be pleased to see their daddy. Ellen has started to turn sour of late and I certainly won't miss the little post-boy.

ELLEN HARBIRD

All I could think of was, why me? I knew something was amiss when Mr Newman came to find me, and asked me to go with him to no. 73. Maud made to come too, but he said please could she wait at home, as he had something of importance to say to me, and it would be better if he could talk to me on my own. I thought, something has happened to Geoffrey. Mr Newman looked so serious, I thought, please don't let John have done something stupid. I said, 'I can't leave the house, I have work to do, will it wait?' No, apparently it wouldn't. I felt quite fearful, and said, 'It's not John?' No, not John. I followed him down the road, and there in the kitchen were Annie and Frances. 'Just tell me what has happened,' I said. 'I can take it.' Well, I nearly couldn't.

I sat down at the table, not moving or saying anything. Annie had her arm round my shoulders. I didn't cry. I just sat. I had so many emotions. I simply couldn't take it in. I heard myself say, 'But he is married to *me*.' How did I not know? Am I such a fool? 'Where is John?' I said, although I knew he was not due home until later. I looked round at their anxious faces.

'I am sorry. I did not mean to cause you all so much trouble. Why would he do such a thing? Where is his wife? Am I married? Who will want us now?'

Annie hugged me.

JOSEPH NEWMAN

We made the decision between us to tell Ellen as soon as possible. Once Christine had found the house, we knew it wouldn't be long before the news got out. I thought she had taken it pretty well, no tears, but Annie said she was in shock. We took Ellen back home, where Maud and John were waiting for her. John was horrified at the news, but at the same time thrilled at the thought that Geoffrey could be arrested at any moment. I went upstairs to tell Mother. She is good in a crisis and I thought her steady attitude would serve us all well. She showed no surprise but rallied straight away, going downstairs to find Ellen, who was talking nineteen to the dozen, and pacing the kitchen. She kept on repeating herself. Mother told me to go to her drawer and find her sleeping draught, which she personally administered to Ellen. Annie took her upstairs to her room, where the poor woman fell at once into a troubled doze, holding on to Maud's hand. Annie instructed Maud to call her as soon as Ellen awoke. John was pacing up and down, longing to 'set the law on him'. I said, 'This is not something for you to decide, it is up to your ma and the other injured party.' We are just here to help, and see how best to resolve this terrible situation.

There was no sign that night of Geoffrey – indeed, under the circumstances, I would have been surprised to see him. We all stayed up talking. None of us fancied being alone, and we didn't know quite what to do. Who did the house belong to? Not Ellen, in any event. Annie said, 'We will have to look for new lodgings. I had better go and tell Olive and the girls what has occurred. We all need to keep working, and we all need a roof.'

The next day saw Ellen get up and just carry on. She said she didn't know what else to do. John wanted to go and find Geoffrey and sort it out, but was persuaded to return to his job and say nothing to a soul. Annie and the girls continued with their work and Miss Olive left to see the author in Chelsea. Apart from the lack of Geoffrey, the day started much like another. I went to work too, and came home via the Finborough. There was no sign of the yellow waistcoat, which I must say was a relief, as I was not at all sure how to confront Geoffrey, and I am not good with conflict. I stopped off to see Frances, to keep her up to date with events, which was to say that nothing had changed.

'You will have to go to Camden Town, and speak with Mrs H. (the first),' she said brightly. 'If the police are to be called, it would be better sooner rather than later, when he might have made good his escape.'

I was not at all sure the task should fall to me. After all, I am not a relative, only the lodger. But Frances seemed determined.

'Ellen needs action, not pity. I can't go, I have two tarts in the oven. You need to find out what Mrs H. intends to do. It is always better in these circumstances to get in first, not end up on the back foot.'

Frances seems to know a lot about the vagaries of relationships. As far as I know she is single and not courting. Maybe she is a reader of sensational fiction, and has picked up a few tips. I could certainly do with some. Then she looked up at me, as though she had been struck with a bolt.

'Of course,' she said. Ellen doesn't need you, she needs Hildebrand.'

JOHN TAYLOR

Joseph came home in a great state. 'We need to act fast, John. Can you deliver a very special message, straight away?' I said, of course, where to? It seems that Frances learnt all her skills in the kitchen from a barrister, called Mr Hildebrand Moore. He has given up the legal game, but Frances was absolutely certain that he is the one person who could help and advise Ma. She puts great store by him, and appears to think that if anyone can sort the mess out, it will be him.

I put my cap back on before taking Joseph's message, so it would be official. The address was for an agency in West End. I said, 'It's an office, it may be closed now.' Joseph said, 'This is for your ma, John. You must wait until it opens, or until someone can give you a home address for Mr Moore. Can I trust you?' Of course he could. I felt like a hero or something, saving Ma.

I was in luck. Mr Moore was still working. In fact he was the last one in the office, and told me he was about to leave to sort out supper. I gave him the note. He paced up and down while reading it. 'You live at no. 53, and you know Frances?' I nodded. 'It sounds like your mother could do with a hand. You know a crime has been committed?' I nodded again. 'Supper can wait. This is a call to arms. I have my bicycle outside, I will meet you back at home.'

I was impressed — he was speed itself. He locked up the office and disappeared down a side street to re-emerge on the smartest roadster I had ever seen. He gave a cheery wave and pedalled off double-quick down the street, leaving me to make my own way back. It is like a proper detective story now. If only Ma wasn't involved I would be quite excited.

HILDEBRAND MOORE

Ada tells me that I bore too easily. She is quite right of course, it has always been a failing, but it also means that I am a quick responder, alert for new excitements. I had often wondered how my *protégée* was progressing in the kitchen, but I had assumed that if our paths crossed again it would be to discuss the finer points of a *béchamel* rather than the wiles of a bigamist. The young man who came to see me impressed on me that speed was key, so I decided to postpone my supper and bicycle instantly over to my old stamping ground.

I must say, the old place had gone rather downhill. The paint was peeling on the columns and there was a slight air of gloom, with little sign of life through the windows. I thought to call on Frances first so I completely understood the story before making myself known at 53. She was just serving up, and, loath as I am to sing my own praises, I have done a fine job. A *blanquette de veau* was making its way towards a dumbwaiter, and it looked in peak condition, The veal was creamy, with a velvety glaze, and completely white, which I had constantly stressed. But first things first.

Frances gave me a potted version of events up the road, stressing how much she liked Ellen Harbird, and how much she disliked Geoffrey, who apparently favours a yellow waistcoat. I said a yellow waistcoat should have alerted anyone to trouble right from the start. She heartily agreed. I was also made aware of the other residents, Annie Walsh and Joseph Newman, who I gather are friends and supporters of the distressed Ellen. They are all looking to me to 'put things right'.

I did not want to talk myself out of a job, so to speak, but I did feel I should say to Frances that I was now director of an advertising agency, and had never been a policeman. The reply was brisk (she has obviously taken to her new post with relish). I could turn my hand to most things, and had I not been, as far as she recalled, a barrister when we first met? In her opinion my voice alone would go a long way to calming down the first Mrs H. and rattling Geoffrey, and if I could produce some 'legal terms' in the course of the conversation, that would 'be of assistance' too. Assistance how? I pointed out that he has probably made off, but I was happy to speak to Ellen Harbird, the police and the kitchen sink if necessary. Should she deem it a good idea I could also fit in a visit to Camden. Frances seemed not to notice my sarcasm and said that was all she asked. By the by, did I think she had put too much salt in the sauce? I must say, even I found it hard to concentrate on salt when considering the task before me.

Just as I was leaving the kitchen, who should appear but Arthur, looking very sleek. He was a very mouldy specimen when Mr Amery found him, now he would not look out of place in a Bond Street pet emporium. I congratulated Frances on his appearance but she had no time for general chatter and I was briskly shown the door with instructions to 'keep her informed'. I know my place.

ELLEN HARBIRD

I wasn't sure what to think when a man with a bicycle came to the door. Sent by Frances, he said. I thought he was the police, but he spoke and looked like a proper gentleman, so I asked him inside. The first thing he noticed was the ginger jar on the mantlepiece. 'I remember that ornament. Mrs Amery swept it to the floor during a dusting manoeuvre. So glad you still have a use for it.' He then explained how he had lived as a lodger in our house, and had been summoned to help me with my problem. 'We need to talk,' he said (although he hadn't stopped since he walked in). 'Are your friends upstairs? It would be helpful, I think, if they listened in too, good for support.'

We all gathered together in Annie's room. The gentleman, 'Please call me Hildebrand' Moore, admired a skirt she was cutting, and said his business partner would be thrilled to hear a lady of such talents was now working from what had been her old room. He could see any lady in London wanting to own such a dress, surely the lace could only be from Paris? I could swear Annie blushed. He shook Joseph by the hand as he came in, and then said, 'And now to business.'

He explained how he had worked in the law, that I had clearly been ill used, and that the proper course of action was to involve the police. I said was that the only option? A court case would see my name in the newspaper and everyone would know how I had been tricked and made to look a fool. Mr Moore said that Geoffrey serving a prison sentence, with a dose of hard labour, might encourage me to feel more cheerful. I said, I just needed to forget about it. Mr Moore said that was all very well, but where had I thought to live, and on what? I hadn't had the time to think. He said he was of a mind to go to the address in Camden and see if he could talk to Mrs H. (the first). He would ask Ada Reeve, his partner in the business, to accompany him, as he felt that a lady's presence could be of use. Did we agree?

Well, we did. It would have been hard not to. He also asked Joseph to accompany him, as it would be helpful to have someone to hand who could recognize Geoffrey. He held my hand before leaving. 'Ellen, may I call you that? I shall do anything I can to assist you at this difficult time. Wait until I return. If you hear from Geoffrey meantime, tell him you have employed a barrister. Here is a card.' He nodded, said he would 'see himself out' and disappeared down the stairs, with Joseph in tow.

Joseph glanced back as he left, and for the first time since the news, we all smiled.

ADA REEVE

If I had to pick out one thing that I find particularly endearing about Hildebrand, it is the fact that he thinks I am game for anything – and, of course, he is right. When he appeared at my door and said he needed my help to sort out a bigamist, I hardly turned a hair. 'Well, naturally,' I replied, 'and will it require my shorthand skills too?' 'Excellent thought, as usual,' he laughed. 'This might well be a moment when it would be useful to keep a track of the conversation.'

He had a cab standing by outside. Seated inside was a quiet, polite middle-aged man, who he introduced as 'Mr Newman, a friend of Frances'. On our way over to one of the more dismal roads in Camden Town, I was filled in on the tale of woe. I was very struck by the way Frances had managed to contact Hildebrand, and most entertained to hear that a dressmaker had taken over my old room. Hildebrand is keen on detail, so by the time we arrived I had an exact picture of Ellen, Annie and the dress (yellow silk, oak-leaf embroidery with overwork in Parisian lace). I also had a deep foreboding about the man with the yellow waistcoat.

The door was opened by a rather determined-looking woman, with the attitude of one expecting a confrontation. She glanced over her shoulder into the room behind. Hildebrand took control. 'Delighted. Mrs Harbird, I assume? Might we come in?'

Without waiting for an answer, he walked straight past her through the hallway, and into the room. There, standing by the fireplace, looking very much at home and still sporting the yellow waistcoat, was the infamous Geoffrey. The gentleman seemed entirely at ease. He smiled at us both, put his arm around the lady who had opened the door and said, 'I think you have met Mrs Harbird. Mr Newman, how nice, and your mother? Now, I don't think I have had the pleasure?' And he waited for us to introduce ourselves.

JOSEPH NEWMAN

Well, it didn't take long for Mr Moore to take the wind out of Geoffrey's sails. Half an hour later I could see that it was all over for him. He had sat down in a chair looking more like a man about to face hard labour (which he was) than the life and soul of the Finborough. He tried to bluff it out, and it was soon apparent that he had bought his way back into the first Mrs H.'s affection with promises of the house at 53 and a new windfall. Ellen had been dismissed as a person of no interest or influence, to be evicted from the premises as soon as.

Mr Moore instructed Miss Reeve to take notes, and it was a real pleasure to see the discomfort in Geoffrey's eyes as she took out her notebook and began taking down the conversation. Mr Moore interrupted Geoffrey every now and then to throw in a remark of his own. 'Please note, Miss Reeve, that Mr Harbird admits entering into a second marriage, while there is clear evidence before us that his first wife is alive and well.' 'Again, Miss Reeve, the bond of the first marriage is clearly established by the presence of two children.' He held up a hand and apologized to Geoffrey. 'One moment, if you please,

Mr Harbird. Miss Reeve, the second marriage was witnessed, and took place in England, the injured party unaware that any misdeed was taking place.'

So it went on, while Miss Reeve scribbled away furiously. Geoffrey started to look increasingly uneasy. Then Mr Moore issued a final aside: 'There is a clear case of felony here, and if the party is convicted he should be kept in penal servitude for a term not exceeding, say — seven years.'

Geoffrey was the colour of his waistcoat. 'Now,' said Mr Moore beaming at him, 'there are two ways we can go about this . . .'

ELLEN HARBIRD

I am still in shock. Events have moved so quickly, and I seem to have gone from being a married drudge with not a penny to my name, to a single woman of means. Mr Moore returned to see me, accompanied by Joseph and a young lady who he introduced as his business partner. They had found Geoffrey about to settle back into a house in Camden Town, with his first wife. Mr Moore had apparently explained to Geoffrey the error of his ways, and how the legal profession did not look kindly on 'bigamists with yellow waistcoats'. He had given Geoffrey a choice. The full force of the law, which would undoubtedly end with a lengthy term of hard labour, or the opportunity to provide for both of his wives, and leave his children with a father.

Joseph had been sent out on the pretext of searching out a policeman, while Geoffrey pondered on his lot. He has apparently agreed to sell the house, and divide the monies between myself and his first wife. He is also to give me a quarter of his second 'windfall', if it comes about. Mr Moore showed me a paper signed to this effect, and witnessed by his first wife and Joseph. Mr Moore says he thinks that will be for the best, as if Geoffrey 'goes down', he sees no one being particularly served. Geoffrey was forced to agree that Mr Moore would act as executor and take charge of the sale and the funds. I asked what the first Mrs Harbird thought to all this. 'Well, if you'll forgive me, it's a case of a har-bird in the hand, so to speak. She has her husband back, more money than before and an agreement that she will receive the bulk of the second little windfall. What is there not to like, Ellen?' He put is so well, that I actually began to think how lucky I was to have met Geoffrey, and that really things could not have turned out better. We will all have to move, but not until a sale is completed, which gives us time to decide what to do and where to go. In the meantime I shall continue to run the house, and take the rents as before, except this time I will be the one keeping the money.

I thanked them all. Annie kissed me, and John shook Mr Moore by the hand. It was like a party. I asked him if he would like a cup of tea but he declined, saying he rather wanted to go and see Frances to discuss various matters, and Miss Reeve was keen to catch up with Arthur. We all gathered round the front door and waved them off. Joseph smiled and said, 'Don't fret, Ellen, everything will turn out for the best.'

For once the stairs in the enterprise didn't seem quite so steep.

GOING UP

The Great Wheel came down in 1906. Ellen, John, Maud and Joseph cheered as the last cogs were removed. It was, as Ellen noted, the moment that Geoffrey was expunged from her life.

Hildebrand ensured a good sale, but Ellen's fortunes had already taken a turn for the better. Joseph had asked her to marry him, and she agreed on a promise that he had no other wives that he was aware of, and that they would move to a new area and start again. A smaller lodging house was purchased in Wandsworth. Annie Walsh became their first lodger. John stayed on to lodge in Chelsea. His friendship with Olive remained just that and he continued to work for the post office.

Ada and Hildebrand decided to employ Olive, and her sense of style and eagerness to work did much to enhance the office. Soon she could be found taking the notes at meetings with a very reasonable 80 wpm, learnt at a course paid for by Ada, who believed passionately that women should be taken seriously in the workplace. Ada followed the speeches of Mrs Pankhurst, and helped with the printing and distribution of leaflets, taking a great pride in the name suffragette. She was, however, worried when the movement took a radical turn, thinking that their actions would damage the cause.

Ada also had plans for Maud, but as she grew up Maud expressed a desire to work in a department store, and secured a place in Harrods, which was by then the largest store in the world, and boasted the distinction of being the first shop in London equipped with a moving staircase. Maud worked in accessories and entertained Annie in the evenings with descriptions of the customers and their purchases.

Hildebrand decided that he could not manage without Frances, and she became his cook. His dinner parties became legendary. The two would spend days deciding on themes and sauces, pushing each other to further extravagences. Ada called them the 'odd couple'. Mr Arthur Fin and Frances were not to be parted either, and a suitable chair was provided so Mr Fin could continue to scan for mice from an advantageous height.

The house is now sold to a Mr Albert Warmbath, a chiropodist, who is looking to run his practice from home. He takes in lodgers, a Mr Arthur Hagley, motor cleaner and washer in a car production factory, who has a wife, Rose, and four children. The eldest, young Arthur, is sixteen and works with his father in the factory as a motor tyre repairer. There is also a widow, Jane Wood, who works from the house as a dressmaker. They have several rooms each, which is a step up, and they share the bathroom. The Hagleys have enhanced the cooking arrangements with a spirit stove, kettle and frying pan which are kept in their 'parlour'.

The new keyholders

THE LIFE AND SOLE
WINTER 1907

ALBERT WARMBATH
Aged forty-two years, chiropodist

I always say to my clients that I like to think of myself as a 'saver of soles'. I find that a little joke at the start of a consultation puts them at their ease. It could have gone either way. My name has been a source of humour as long as I can remember, and my choice of occupation has not helped. As we shook hands, my new lodger (who happens to work in the car trade) opened proceedings with a light jest, 'At least I know where to turn for a toe.' These are the sort of remarks that come with the territory. I must have heard them all, but then I decided to get in first, so to speak, and sometimes half an hour cutting a corn can turn into a riot of amusement. Originally I had added the words 'saver of soles' underneath my name to the brass plaque on the door, but this attracted more attention from the Bible fraternity, eager to point out my spelling mistake, than customers in need of a nail operation, and I have had to redo the sign, so now it is just my name and profession. A pity really.

I have sometimes thought that I could supplement my income by providing foot jokes to the novelty cracker industry, and to that end I sometimes jot down a few. If I have had a particularly trying day I glance through them, and they never fail to make me chuckle. I particularly like a pun: 'The ballerina had to give up. Dancing was tu-tu painful on her feet.' That sort of thing. The fact of the matter is that I can't bear to watch ballet. Where other people see beauty and grace I see toes buckled and bleeding from going *en pointe*. I cannot put a distance between the fantasy and the reality. When I walk down the street it is feet rather than faces that catch my attention. A pair of tight boots, or a high heel, makes me wince. If only fashionable ladies realized the harm that a pointed toe can bring about, they would clomp about in boots – except they don't. So I am in demand.

Considering how much time I spend holding a woman's foot, it is remarkable how little success I have had over the years with the ladies. I have always been told that a lady prizes a sense of humour over looks. In my own personal experience this has not been the case. My jokes, which always seem to elicit a smile, do not result in further shows of emotion. I am thanked and paid, but the intimacy that occurs as I gently caress and doctor their toes does not seem to extend to further acquaintance. I do not have many friends. Not everyone shares my interest in the foot and, after I have explored a joke or two, I find that my social skills peter out and I usually leave any gathering with my conversation intact.

I don't know when my interest in feet took hold. At school during history classes I always took notice in the small social aspects of the past. I found myself reading about Hippocrates and his scrapers, which led on to learning about the medieval practitioners who coated corns with swine dung, and then I made it my focus to collect trivial information to entertain my fellow pupils. I would hold their attention with a few facts – Napoleon's best friend was his corn-cutter, the Duke of Wellington had no time for any soldier who complained of problem feet, thinking they deserved it – were two of many. I took to looking at drawings of shoes that had been adapted for bunions and made illustrations with my own ideas. What had started off as a means of attracting attention became a fascination.

This led, sadly, to fewer friends. Boys who had laughed with me at my knowledge began to avoid me, and then the jokes started. By the time I left I had become an introverted young man, with a passion.

This house was very run down and rather dated when I moved in. I have engaged in modernizing the property. I have been down to Crapper's shop in the King's Road and ordered a new bathroom. The salesman tried to talk me into installing a shower above the bath – apparently they are all the rage in America – but I drew the line, instead agreeing to take a bulk order of toilet paper that was on special offer, and a seven-piece accessory kit, which included everything from a tumbler holder to a towel bar. Solid brass, nickel-plated. Customers often ask if they can 'avail themselves' and I think that these are the sort of touches that impress. I have been upgrading the gas lights and am wondering about a new gas cooker. The range looks like a veritable antique. I have been told that you can rent one from the gas company, which may suit.

I am installing a new kitchen sink, and tiling. You won't know the old place soon. I uncovered and subsequently threw away an ancient *découpage* tray (it reminded me of something my mother might have done), but kept an old ginger jar I found hidden at the back of a cupboard. The lid was broken, but I am using the base as a spoon holder. I feel like a newly-wed.

I am taking in lodgers, and even they are a reflection of the modern times we are living in. Mr Hagley is a motor cleaner and washer in a car production factory! His eldest son, also Arthur, works there too, as a motor tyre repairer. Who would ever have thought it? I would love to attempt to drive a car, I am interested in mechanical design. Rose, his wife, looks after the three younger children, but is also going to act as cook, for a concession on the rent. This came about rather by accident than design, but Mr Hagley assures me that his Rose 'can knock the socks off anyone, when it comes to a pot roast', so I have agreed a trial. It certainly suits me not to engage in hiring servants. Rose is going to look out for a maid, so all in all we are getting the household sorted. As soon as we are all safely in, I shall start to advertise my practice. My old stomping ground was in the suburbs, too far for my patients to travel in, so I shall build up my list again. I am not concerned. I am to feet as Crapper is to plumbing.

ARTHUR HAGLEY
Aged forty years, motor cleaner and washer

I think we have landed on our feet (see, I can't stop now I've started). Rose got quite cross the other day, saying she had heard enough, but it is true. Our landlord is a bachelor, which I prefer;

we have had our fill of landladies, who always glance down at the family with at the best a look of disapproval or more often worse. I remember one who felt it incumbent on her to remark that children 'even at their best are just small people with criminal faces', which I felt excessive.

I had one of my 'flashes' when I came to look around. I knew that Mr Warmbath had just moved in, and the house was in the process of redecoration, so as I was looking at our rooms I asked right out if he had employed a cook yet. Well, the upshot of that is I have got Rose a job, and an extra room thrown in, so now she has a parlour. This is something she has always wanted. Over the years we have been crammed into spaces where the chances of swinging a cat were low. Rose says we are very lardy dardy now, and I have purchased a new spirit stove and pan, so we can have a fry-up round the table. Mr W. seemed very relaxed about the children, saying it 'would bring some life to the place'. That's for sure. There is a dressmaker upstairs, who has three rooms all to herself. She does a bit of work, but seems to have enough money to make ends meet, and greeted me very pleasantly, holding out her hand to shake young Arthur's before rustling about in a tin and giving the youngsters a barley sugar each. Nothing like a sweet to oil the wheels. Mr W. has had a new bathroom fitted. I paid extra for a Friday bath. The children have never had a real bath, they just looked at it with amazement. Rose had tears in her eyes. No more tins or bathhouses for us. The Hagleys are on the up.

ROSE HAGLEY
Aged forty-three years
Wife to ARTHUR

Arthur is one of those men who always sees the glass as half-full, and it seems for once he may be right. Usually when he comes back to say he has secured new lodgings for us I find each one more upsetting than the last. I have put up with 'just a bit of damp', when the condensation flowed down the walls, mice that have run over the top of the blanket without a by-your-leave, and . . . well, don't ask me about the privvies. I have seen it all. The children have all been covered in bites since they were babes. Bed bugs are the worst. You can smash a mattress until the stuffing falls out, and soap every inch of the bedstead and still in the night you could scratch the skin right off your legs. Anyway, it seems to have done none of them any harm. They are the liveliest bunch you could find. I don't want to say too lively, but when we enter the school gates I have seen teachers mouth to each other 'The Hagleys are here', as if the day had just got worse.

Anyway, on the strength of Arthur's new job, and the extra coming in now from young Arthur, we were able to look for new rooms. I wasn't expecting anything. When Arthur came back and told me I would be having my own parlour, I just laughed, and then he said 'and bath'. I said, 'You really are having me on' – but he wasn't. Mr Warmbath is a corn-cutter, and has only just moved in. He has redecorated. I didn't know anyone did that – our rooms too. We have three! I have wanted a parlour for I don't know how long. Young Arthur will sleep in the room at night, and the three smallest will share. Arthur and me will have a room to ourselves. 'None of that nonsense,' I said when he showed it to me with a cheery wink. I felt sorry when his face fell, but I'm pushed out. The bathroom is new. The taps are so shiny I could see my face in them. I am to do a bit of cooking for Mr W., which will suit me, as the children are all off at school in the day. There is a lady upstairs who has three rooms all to herself, but Arthur says she is all right.

I told them all that we will have to be on our best, and I think they understood. I don't want complaints. I have been given the job of looking for a maid. I can ask my friend Kate; she is a worker. Yes, the Hagleys are definitely on the up.

ARTHUR HAGLEY

Rose is a bit older than me. I met her when I had just turned twenty. I won't say it was love at first sight, but there was something about her. Wasn't that bothered about me at first, but I kept at it. I knew she was the one. It's the way she's interested in everything. People, a dog, gardens, always something that she wants to talk about. Going for a walk with Rose she'll point out things that I've missed, but that've caught her eye. She's a looker. It's always, 'Look at this, look at that, over there – ahh, you missed it.' I thought, 'She'll do.' I could never get bored with Rose. Turn her hand to anything. Never complains, no matter what I throw at her, and it's not been easy. Can't imagine a day without her. To see her face when I showed her the parlour gave me more pleasure than I can remember for a long time. I brought some flowers back yesterday. They went straight into a jug on the middle of the table, as though she had done it every day of our married life.

I still can't quite believe we've got the rooms. I was just going past the house at the right time. I saw this painter going in, then I realized he was a friend of mine. He said, 'You want to get in here. The gentlemen's looking for lodgers, but he hasn't put the advertisement in the paper yet.' I went straight up. I thought he would take one look and show me the door, but we started talking and I told him about my job with the cars and, would you believe it, he thinks cars are the future! I was there chatting with him for about half an hour (he likes a laugh, too), and then he says he'd better show me the rooms, see if they were to my satisfaction. Were they.

I am going to see if I can get Mr W. a drive. He has expressed an interest in coming up and looking at the cars being built. That won't be a problem, I get on well with everyone up there, and the foreman will be chuffed to show a gentleman round the works. Young Arthur is well in too, and has a responsible job changing the tyres. Keeps busy – tyres don't last long, always bursting. He is apprentice one day a week to one of the panel-beaters, so shouldn't be too long before he has a real trade in the car business. I just know it's the future, and that ours will be bound up in it.

ROSE HAGLEY

I met Arthur when he was in his early twenties. So sure of himself, always happy. It wasn't love at first sight, but I thought he'll do, he'll look out for me. We haven't had much luck with the money, but we have been blessed with each other. I know that Arthur will never let me down. He's there when I need him. Loves the children. Some men are at a loss with children. When they look at their family all they see are mouths on legs. Not Arthur. He takes them out, points out the names of the ducks in the park, plays with them for pleasure, not as a chore. He'd rather be with us than down the pub. Can't imagine a day without him. We're known as 'The Hagleys', a troupe. Young Arthur has been taken on at the factory. When they come home I hear all about the motor cars. Occasionally we've been out on a Sunday and Arthur spots one of their vehicles on the road. We all wave – the owners must think we're mad – the little ones get very excited. Once the mechanic waved back and tooted the horn. They bring their cars back to the factory for cleaning and polishing. That's Arthur's job. He polishes them up before they leave to go to the showroom too. He never liked horses. His mum was run over by a horse and cart as it was leaving the local barracks. The doctor didn't set the bones back right and after that she never walked properly. Arthur was only small, but he never forgot the fear – always puts the children behind him when we're waiting to cross the road. Although I'm not sure which is the more dangerous, horses or the motors. Neither seem to pay much heed to me, that's for sure. The bicyclists and the drivers scorch up and down Finborough Road. We have a motor omnibus and, this year, motor cabs too. Maybe Arthur is on the money. Cars will be our future, so I had better learn to love them.

ALBERT WARMBATH

I have not had much experience of children. No brothers or sisters, and obviously none of my own. It has come somewhat as a surprise to me that I have started to feel rather envious of the Hagleys. They seem so perfectly content to be with each other. When I have had my supper I hear them downstairs, chattering away to each other, the little ones playing games. Sometimes Rose's voice rises above the general cacophony, telling them to 'pipe down'. They aren't saints by any means – the other day I found the youngest, Edward, hiding under the table in my parlour, apparently in a bid to conceal himself from his sisters – but they are smiling, happy children, and I find myself looking forward to seeing them. On Sunday they all get dressed in their best and go out for the day. If the weather is nice they might take sandwiches, if it's raining they head off to the museums. Rose tells me they enjoy 'just walking', as there's always so much to see. When I hear the door closing I experience an emotion that I can only describe as sad. The ensuing silence seems to emphasize my bachelor state. I thought once of asking if I could come along too, but it was clearly an inappropriate idea. I dismissed the thought as soon as it had crossed my mind, but it got me thinking. Would my life be more satisfying if I had a wife?

When I was a young man I assumed, with the arrogance of youth, that marriage would naturally come about. Yet here I am, in my forties, on my own. I am content. My work fills the day, and I have conversation enough, although some might think it lacked variety. I leave the house a few evenings a month. I go out occasionally to a concert, and have a couple of friends who include me in their society. So why has this dissatisfaction with my lot come about ?

Maybe it is the new house. It appears to me that I have developed a need to share. I am not entirely naive. I see a lot of ladies in my day-to-day work. Many would not enhance my life, indeed the reverse, and yet . . . I can see myself, arm linked through arm, beside a Mrs Warmbath.

These new thoughts have started to take hold, but I am at loss as how to achieve my aim.

I have already established that I am not going to find my soulmate by waiting until they knock on the door with a troublesome bunion. I can see now that it is not a profession that lends itself to romance. I must rely on my wits, and put myself out into society to increase my chances of success. To this end I have decided to put aside my book of jokes and the cracker ambition to concentrate solely on the Mrs Warmbath enterprise. I shall compose a list of amusements and venues where it might be possible to strike up a conversation without it seeming peculiar. I can also add notes analysing my thoughts on the possible outcome and then decide which ones seem the most likely to bear fruit — so to speak — before striking out. This is not the time for cold feet!

ROSE HAGLEY

I have noticed a change in Mr W. He is a man who likes routine. At supper he normally has an evening paper which he might glance at, or the small notebook containing his jokes — he likes a joke — he reads through them carefully, sometimes pausing so he can add a new one to the list. I asked him about them once and he said that was to be his 'retirement fund', which I thought odd.

Anyway, now he has taken to asking me questions, quite personal ones really, but I don't mind, I can see he is really interested. He asked me yesterday how I met Arthur – 'was it love at first sight?' Then tonight what I had first found attractive in him – 'was it his looks?' He has also given up writing in the little lined book and replaced it with a file. I see him putting in advertisements and pamphlets from theatres and galleries, and he seems to be collecting cards from restaurants. He is up to something.

I asked Arthur what he thought, but he lacks a curiosity in the goings-on of people. Says he has enough to worry about with all of us, and not to 'bother Mr W.' 'Don't be so dull,' I said. I am going to keep a look-out and find out what is distracting him. He has been glancing at himself in the mirror more of late, so if I didn't know better I would say it was a woman, but I have never seen him show any interest in ladies, and he sees enough of them. As I said to Arthur, if Marie Lloyd skirt-danced up the stairs he would be more likely to enquire about her welted soles than her flexible legs. Arthur, hopeless as usual, paying no attention, replied, 'Who's skirt-dancing up the stairs?', as though it was an everyday occurrence. He can be so daft. I shall discuss it with Kate when she comes tomorrow, maybe she's noticed something I've missed. She will certainly show more interest.

ALBERT WARMBATH

I have to say that I feel I am doing rather well with my new venture. I am well along the road with ideas and as I go about at the weekend I have begun to make a collection of pamphlets from various locations that I can study at my leisure.

I have also found Rose a good source of information. It seemed silly to ignore the couple who have inspired my quest. I have not had time alone with Arthur Hagley recently, but I feel he too would be worth quizzing on the subject of matrimony. Clearly, I do not want to enlighten them as to what I have in mind, but I think I am canny enough to be able to conduct some light-hearted questioning without arousing their interest. Rose seems only too happy to tell me about her initial meetings with Arthur, and I was pleased to note that I do not need to seek out the 'lightning bolt of love', so to speak. I was nervous of this aspect of the proceedings. Of course in the past I have met ladies I have found attractive, but I have never been smitten in the way you sometimes hear. I have been glancing through a couple of romantic novelettes (usually, I believe, the favoured reading source of the younger woman), but I cannot say that I have found them particularly useful. *Three Weeks*, which was recommended to me by the local bookseller as a work of erotic romance, made me wonder as to the sanity of both the seller and the authoress, Miss Glyn. I gather she has written many novels and even inspired some doggerel verse. The story revolved round the assignations of a nobleman and 'a lady', who turns out to be very much not a lady, and married to a Russian king. The book consists of a lot of lustful glances, and some fumbling. It was not helpful, in fact nearly put me off the entire project. Talking to Rose has put me back on track.

ROSE HAGLEY

I knew something was up. Kate was taking particular care dusting round Mr W.'s room and found a book she did not like the look of. Her reading is poor so I got no further, but I have instructed her to keep on dusting, and we shall soon see what's what. A man doesn't need too many secrets. Maybe Arthur should take him up to the factory for the promised 'look round', except I know they would probably end up talking pistons and spark plugs, and we will be no further forward. Let's see what he chats about this evening, and maybe I can ask a question or two of my own. I'll do his favourite liver casserole, followed by my custard. That always brings on a smile.

ALBERT WARMBATH

OPERATION MRS WARMBATH: IDEAS AND ACTION

Walking in the Park

Pros – The Italian Gardens, bandstand and Broad Walk should all make for good opportunities. There is also the boating lake and the Round Pond.

Cons – Weather conditions.

Actions – Would a dog be useful? Ladies seem to show a sympathetic side when it comes to animals. Feeding the pigeons could prove simpler, a good starting point. A brolly?

Attend local suffrage meeting

Pros – Mostly attended by ladies.

Cons – I am nervous of political types, which they undoubtedly are.

Actions – Offer to assist (although not in any violent exchanges).

Travel

Pros – One of my clients was extolling the virtues of a cruise. There is time a-plenty to engage in friendships. She had travelled with her husband on the RMS *Adriatic* to New York. The ship has an indoor swimming pool and a Turkish bath on board.

Cons – Cost. I am not a rich man. It might set a precedent in the mind of the future Mrs Warmbath. Time. A verruca waits for no man.

Actions – Secure brochure. Isle of Wight ferry possibly a cheaper option?

Learn a new sport

Pros – Choice. I could take up anything from bowls to bicycling by joining a club. I would not seem out of place and there are clearly conversations to be had around a hobby.

Cons − I have never been a 'club' man, and am hopeless at all ball games.

Actions − Check in the local paper for possible activities. I spotted a stable on the Kenway Road.

Church

Pros − St Luke's, my local, is well attended. Join the choir?

Cons − I am not a particularly religious man, apart from attending church on a Sunday. I would not like the future Mrs Warmbath to be overly pious. I am a shy singer and usually ignore the request to 'sing up'. The ladies seem to give all their attentions to the Reverend. I heard one seeking his opinion on flower-arranging.

Actions − Ask Reverend Handcock about choral opportunities.

Concerts/art galleries

Pros − Can be attended regardless of time of year or weather conditions. Light-hearted banter can be conducted in the interval. Paintings provide a useful vehicle for discussion.

Cons − I have never talked to anyone either at the theatre or at an exhibition.

Actions − Start to attend our larger art establishments. I shall include museums on the list too, as I can see striking up an intimacy around the exhibits should not be impossible.

I shall also make a short list of my attributes, and the type of person I am seeking. I cannot believe I have waited so long. As soon as I have done my research I will have to work out a timetable for the outings. I can see the next few weeks being very busy. Rose may have to be flexible with my supper time, but I cannot see that posing a difficulty. I am giddy with ideas, and may even invest in a new coat and hat. Arthur Hagley has asked me along to see the car production. Why not? He is enquiring of his manager as to the best time, and I shall 'book myself out'. After all, I am foot-loose and – at the moment – fiancée-free!

ARTHUR HAGLEY

I might as well have given in when Rose first started going on. She is absolutely determined that poor old Mr W. has women on his mind. I said, 'So what? As far as I know it's not illegal.'

Rose said that it will affect us, as we have it easy at the present. There is apparently no knowing how our circumstances could change with Mr W. under the thumb of a wife. I stayed mum, that's best when Rose has a plan. Rose has instructed me to take him out to the factory for a morning and, while we engage in discussing the benefits of the motor, I am to attempt to find out if he has ambitions in that direction. I know whatever I find out won't be enough for Rose. This task may be beyond me. Cleaning cars – yes. Talking to my landlord about his girls – save me. Anyway, I have done as she asked, and we are going off together next week. Mr W. seems really pleased, and me and young Arthur are looking forward to it too. I just wish I didn't have Rose on my back.

ALBERT WARMBATH

Well, I must say that Arthur rather underplayed his hand. The business off Ladbroke Grove is palatial (twenty-eight acres, the foreman told me) and, as you might expect, owned by an Earl! The reception had columns, frescoes and stained glass windows etched with the Earl's coat of arms. I must say I was rather disappointed not to see said Earl overseeing the assembly, but

I suppose he cannot be in all places, and I gather they have a showroom in Longacre. I did see a illustration of him at the wheel of one the motors. The small plaque on the frame confirming his identity as Lord Shrewsbury & Talbot. He has named the motors Talbot, which I thought snappy if lacking in imagination. Arthur was busy polishing up a red two-seater. I sat in the seat and imagined Mrs Warmbath and myself motoring off for a day by the sea. Young Arthur never seemed to stop — if he wasn't on wheel-changing he was seeing to the tools and equipment used by the panel-beaters. The machine tools were very modern and the whole place flooded with light. Apparently they make about sixty cars a month. I told young Arthur he was not only witnessing but helping to build our future. I could see for once I had said the right thing — earlier on I had attempted a tyre joke, and it had fallen very flat. He has not inherited Arthur's sense of fun. His father introduced me to some of his fellow workers, including one man who said he had seen some designs for airships! I cannot recall enjoying a morning more. I did not want to outstay my welcome, but it seemed the least I could do was to buy Arthur a beer for his trouble before leaving for home. He said he would complete the final polish and meet me round the corner at The Earl of Lonsdale for a half.

Off-site, Arthur appeared somewhat uneasy. I thanked him again, and said how fascinating I had found the experience. He seemed to relax a bit after that, and settled down with his beer, but, while he had been loquacious at the factory, he seemed to lapse into silence. After a moment or two he ventured into small talk. He mentioned it was the Hagleys' wedding anniversary the following month and how happy they both were. Had I never thought of 'tying the knot'? What a piece of luck, the conversation fortuitously taking such a turn. Like an uncoiled spring in a racing Talbot, I quickly stepped in, asking about the advantages of a married life. Did the Hagleys share many common interests? Did children improve the marital state?

How was it they had remained so close, while other couples seemed to grow apart? He seemed to redden up at this close questioning and without replying asked one of his own. Had I ever thought of owning a motor? I tried again, but he muttered this was more Rose's territory than his. He thought some men benefited from the company of a woman, others did not. After this revealing insight he quickly downed his half, got up and said he needed to be back at work, or they would have his guts. Not wanting this on my conscience, we got up, shook hands and went our separate ways.

I know that men are notoriously reluctant to engage in conversations on matrimony, and Arthur is no different. Indeed this is new territory for me. I shall wait no longer. Tonight I complete the proposed timetable, tomorrow I shall start my mission.

ROSE HAGLEY

Well, I knew it. Not only has Arthur lied to Mr W. about our supposed wedding anniversary (which, fingers crossed, he will have forgotten all about by next month), but he has found out absolutely nothing at all. He did say that Mr W. seemed keen to talk about our marriage, asking him the same sort of questions that he put to me. He must have someone in mind. A client maybe.

Oh well, eyes and ears. I can't spend any more time on it today. The Hagleys are going to the Natural History Museum on Sunday. It can get crowded, but with an early start we should be all right.

ALBERT WARMBATH

The weather does not bode well for my first outing. I am going to start off gently and test the water at the Natural History Museum. I enjoy going anyway and know the environment well, so it will not be any hardship. I will start early before the crowds build up.

ROSE HAGLEY

Well, it pays to be a good looker! We got in early and the children were keen to go and see the dinosaurs, but we were waylaid by a couple of elephants. I was just glancing about – when who should I spot but Mr W., who seemed to be studying a drawer of birds' eggs! I could see his attention was not on the eggs, as he was glancing around as if waiting for someone.

I nudged Arthur and said, 'Take the children off to see the whale. I will meet you back here in half an hour.' Arthur said, 'What are you up to now?' But he gathered them up and I saw them disappear towards the back of the museum. I put myself behind a pillar, where I could survey any antics. Mr W. closed the egg drawer and wandered over to the elephant. He still seemed bothered and was glancing around. I didn't have to wait long. A youngish lady appeared by his side and began talking. Mr W. started smiling and responding in a very familiar way. After a moment she waved her arm, and a small girl about eight came over to her side. Mr W. beamed down at the child before gently taking her by the hand and the two of them set off towards the reptile gallery. The lady settled down on a bench to wait for them.

I can't credit it. They are clearly much more than friends. His fancy woman? His child? I wouldn't think he had it in him. I waited for Mr W. and my Arthur to return. Arthur came back first and I filled him in on events. He looked at the lady on the bench. 'Maybe that's his sister,' said Arthur. I don't know where he gets it from. If that's his sister, I'm his maiden aunt. Anyway, I noticed the little girl and Mr W. returning from the gallery, so I got behind the Hagley brood and shooed them all off. As I glanced back I saw the lady looking adoringly into Mr W.'s eyes before placing her arm through his and off they went together up the main staircase, Mr W. still holding the child's hand to steady her on the steps. I know it's his secret family – just wait until I tell Kate.

ALBERT WARMBATH

Not a success, I'm afraid. I was just getting myself into gear, so to speak, and deciding which exhibit would be promising for conversation, when a young lady approached me, with a very bright and friendly 'good morning'. I smiled encouragingly, thinking how my project was turning out to be simpler than I had anticipated.

We chatted away, and I was just getting into my stride, when the lady interrupted with, 'Please let me introduce myself. Mrs Clements. I wonder if you could do me a great service?' She beckoned over a small girl. 'This is my Mary. She loves to see the dinosaurs, but is scared to go in alone, and oddly I am not much better, as I find they stir up dark imaginings. If I place myself on that bench, where I will be in sight, could I ask you to take her through? My husband is away on business, and the weather is so unpromising this seems an ideal outing.' Of course what could I do but say yes? The little girl took my hand and we proceeded to the gallery. I was able to tell her quite a lot about the exhibits, but while I cannot say that our time together was unpleasant, it was not what I had planned.

Mrs Clements was very grateful, and we stayed together for the morning, before going our separate ways. She took a card, saying her husband was always in need of a good chiropodist, and she would make sure he attended my practice. She hoped we would meet again and they would be on the look-out for me in the future. Oh well, it is all good experience, On reflection I think art might prove more productive. I seldom notice young children in art galleries.

—◦◦◦—

The following week I selected the National Gallery for my foray. I have decided that the choice of painting is key. No nudes, no religious oils and, I think, nothing modern. I read in one of my pamphlets about an artist who paints women as cubes. Spanish, I recall. I am certainly not expecting to see anything like that occupying the walls in our great galleries. Turner or Constable will fit the bill. Emotionally fulfilling, yet easy on the eye. I eventually selected the Turner room and sat down on a chair (one of three in a row) to admire the works. I was pleased to note several ladies who seemed to be on their own regarding the pictures.

Well, I had barely been seated for fifteen minutes, when a large man sat down beside me, accompanied by a small, thin woman – presumably his wife. He turned to me as he collapsed on to the chair with the words, 'Warmbath, isn't it? Remember me – Dickenson? Ingrown toenail? May I introduce my wife, Cecilia?' In fact I did remember him. Poor foot hygiene, often the cause. Anyway, I greeted him cordially and enquired about the toe. He was pleased to inform me that the repeated soaking in warm water I had advised along with the Epsom salts had worked wonders. Was I still working up my joke collection? He nudged his wife and asked her if she recalled his visits, and what a lark the appointments had been. She did. The upshot of this encounter was he insisted on us leaving the Turners and 'treating us all to tea'. I have never been so popular. Usually I leave and return after a day having spoken to no one. Now it seems I am the life and sole.

The weather this month has taken a turn for the better, so I have decided to go with one of my original plans and take a turn around the park. I have also decided to throw caution to the wind and procure a dog. My friends the Lombards have a small terrier-type called Percy. I wrote a quick note after work, enquiring if I might take Percy out at the weekend. I used the excuse that I was thinking of owning a dog, and would like to take one out for a test run before committing. I heard back by return, saying that although they were 'surprised' at my request, as I had never shown much enthusiasm for Percy before, they would be only too glad to lend him to me for the morning. He was fond of exercise. Kensington Gardens was his park of choice. If I could collect him before 9.30 a.m. that would be ideal, and they would use the opportunity to go shopping, an activity in which Percy showed little interest. I must say I found it odd to learn that Percy had active thoughts on any subject. He barely gets up when I have been to visit, except to take the odd piece of teacake offered to him by Mrs Lombard.

I turned up on the dot. I had underestimated Percy, who seemed in high spirits. When shown his lead he positively skipped towards the front door. The Lombards caressed him lovingly before wishing us both an invigorating walk. I must say I am always surprised by how perfectly rational people (Mr Lombard is a banker, not prone to exuberance) seem to lapse into idiocy when an animal is involved. They stood at the door rather anxiously I thought, as we set off at a smart pace towards the park, smiling and waving not at me but towards Percy, who did not deign so much as a backward glance. I had thought we would start with a turn around the Memorial, but Percy seemed keen to make for the Round Pond. Happy to oblige. We proceeded in that direction.

There was not a bench or a tree that did not warrant some sort of attention. As we progressed down the path, it was also clear that here was a dog with a strong social side. Couples nodded as we passed by, a young man on a bicycle shouted, 'Hello, Perce' and a lad with a his nurse stopped us for a chat, so that the boy could pat him and make conversation. People of all sorts made enquiries as to the Lombards, concerned for Percy's welfare in unfamiliar hands. I had no idea that London was home to so many dogs, or that their owners would be so keen to stop and exchange trivia relating to their pets and habits.

I may have spoken to some single ladies, or I may not. I saw little chance to broaden the topic beyond the well-being of Percy. 'Isn't he a lovely little dog?' seemed more rhetorical than otherwise.

We returned after several hours, my feet needing a soak and my brain a rest. Percy looked as though he had just started his day. The Lombards said I was welcome to borrow him whenever, as Percy had clearly formed a close attachment to me. On the way home, the young man on the bicycle went past again, shouting, 'Where's Perce?' as he sped by. What is it about me? It comes to something when a dog receives more affection in a few hours than I have attracted in a lifetime.

I did give away some more of my cards, dog-walking taking a toll, it seems, on the feet, so at least business will be flourishing.

ROSE HAGLEY

Mr W. seemed somewhat downcast this evening. Usually he chats away as I serve his supper, but today, although polite as usual, there were not many smiles. Maybe he is missing his daughter.

He did, however, enquire about our anniversary. When was the date? He had a thought that I would like the day off. He could easily manage. I was put in two minds. I am always telling the children that I don't like porkies, but a day off . . . I told Mr W. that I would have to ask Arthur, as he would probably not be able to take time out. He then said, 'Well, why not the whole of a Sunday?' (Usually I get back to make his dinner.) 'A marriage should be celebrated.' I could see he was thinking of his own family. He then moved on to ask about dogs! Did I like them? He said a lot of people seemed to find them companionable. I replied that I didn't give them much thought. Arthur had one when he was a boy, but in truth you don't have a dog when you are moving round with four children. He just nodded and went back to looking at his newspaper. Something then caught his eye and he folded back a page. I turned round just I was leaving the room and boldly asked him right out if he had enjoyed his outing to the Natural History Museum. He look surprised, but not at all put out, replying, 'Oh, yes. It is a place of great interest. Have you been?' 'A couple of weeks back,' I answered. 'It is surprising what you get to see there.' 'It is indeed, Mrs Hagley. I always enjoy the elephants, such gigantic beasts.' I left it there.

ALBERT WARMBATH

Looking back on my morning with Percy, I found I had rather enjoyed the experience. Maybe, if I am not to find Mrs Warmbath, then a dog would be a happy addition to the home. I have never entertained the notion before.

I was looking at my paper over dinner, when an advertisement caught my eye. 'Are you a Lonely Heart? Looking for love and marriage? Would a good husband or a sensitive wife complete the happy home?' Yes, yes — I nearly spoke out loud. As I folded back the page I immediately realized this was the way forward. Why did I not think of it before? So simple. State one's requirements, then sit back and wait for the results. I would not want anyone to find out that I have placed an advertisement, but then why should they? It seems replies would be sent through to the paper. I have nothing to lose and much to gain. I spent the rest of my evening reading through other people's messages so I could get a feeling for the type of information I should include. I was surprised to notice quite a few spelling mistakes, but love, as they say, is blind.

ARTHUR HAGLEY

It is a rare day that I get one over on Rose. I am going to make the most of it. She always thinks that she has a woman's eye when it comes to affairs of the heart. At the moment at home it has been hard to keep her off the subject. Rose has decided that poor Mr W. has a family he is keeping hidden away in another house. She and Kate have been talking of little else, and as each day goes by the story becomes more and more flowery as the two of them work out different tales. When me and young Arthur come home we have to listen to more stories of love lost and love found, until we beg her to keep quiet and sort out tea. I have been told I am 'insensitive' and 'only a man' and 'it takes a woman to understand'. I told her plainly that I didn't want to hear any more rubbish. Then at work today the foreman, Charlie, came up, newspaper in hand. 'You want to read this,' he said and passed over a page of small advertisements. There, under the heading 'Undefeeted Romantic seeks same', was the following:

UNDEFEETED ROMANTIC SEEKS SAME

I am the man to sit at your feet and heel life's scars. My sole is yours. Professional man seeks lady for matrimony. A shapely ankle and a sense of humour invaluable. Own home Earl's Court area. 42 years. Interests include the compilation of jokes, walking of dogs and the arts. Looking for similar.

'Who does that sound like, Arthur? Your chap, isn't it? Foot doctor? Earl's Court?' Apparently Charlie enjoys looking through the lonely heart columns on his break – he did in fact walk out with a widow from Surrey he met through the very same page.

That's it. The questioning, the days out. He is looking for a Mrs Right. I am going to spin this one out. I actually found myself whistling as I worked. I am really looking forward to going home. I didn't mention it to young Arthur. He would spill the beans as soon as we walked in.

———◈———

Rose was still up with Mr W. when we got home. I sat at the table and, hearing her on the stairs, began to read the paper, not looking up when she came through the door. 'I think it's sad, Arthur,' she began as soon as she saw me. 'That poor man, unable to be with the woman he loves.' I carried on reading. 'Living here alone, while she is shunned by family and friends. We live in sad times, Arthur. Are you listening? I thought you had a soft spot for Mr W.? Oh, I forgot to tell you he has remembered our wedding anniversary. I didn't know where to look or what to say. Are you listening? Shift yourself, I need to lay the table. I'm doing some sausages. He doesn't smile like he used to, his mind is elsewhere. Kate says it's a tragedy. Are you listening, Arthur? A tragedy. Can you stop reading that paper, you would think you didn't care. You're too wrapped up with the motors. I see the unhappiness in that man's face every time he looks at our girls. He sees his own daughter, reaching out to hold her father's hand. Two rashers?'

I let her run with it as she laid the table, got out the bread and started frying up some sausages. When she let out a long sigh I could stand it no longer and pushed over the paper towards her. 'I haven't got time to sit down and read. What have you given me this for?' I folded over the page, settled back and read the advertisement out loud. Silence. I gave her the benefit and read it out again. This time I couldn't stop laughing, and young Arthur, who was behind me, joined in. 'Sorry, Rose,' I said. 'I just had to. Mr W. hasn't got a family, secret or otherwise, but he is looking for one.'

ROSE HAGLEY

I didn't know whether to hit him with the newspaper or join in with their laughter. In the end I did neither. Arthur was very pleased with himself, and I could see that from his point of view it was funny. I said, 'Well, I wasn't that far off the mark, be fair. It was an easy mistake. The lady must be a widow, and answered his ad.' Arthur said, 'It's no good, Rose. Admit it, you just don't know. She could be a client or an old acquaintance. Facts, Rose, that's the way.'

Well, we had tea and I sent the three smallest out with young Arthur for a walk before bed. I shan't talk about it any more (except with Kate). Still, it is sad when a man like Mr W. has to resort to an advertisement. He is not bad-looking, has his own house and teeth and is good with feet. There are a lot of women who would thank their stars to find someone like him. Not me, but someone.

ALBERT WARMBATH

It was a busy day. My clients were varied and so were the problems. I prefer that. The hours flew past as athlete's foot made way for a bad callus, followed hard upon by a case of chilblains (tight shoes, again). I was eager to finish, as I had taken delivery of a bundle of letters from the newspaper. It seems there are several ladies who possess a shapely ankle and a sense of humour.

The Hagleys have become very jovial since my outing to the factory. Young Arthur beaming a 'Good morning, Sir' when we passed today on the stairs, and Mr Hagley behind, whistling a very cheery little tune. When I enquired, he said it was called 'The boy I love is up in the gallery', and he had heard it at the music hall. It sounded very amusing. I must go. I shall include it on my list. Even Kate seemed in good humour, almost simpering as she tackled her tasks. All in all, I am pleased to say that I am running a happy ship.

I settled down after work with a small sherry and my notebook, to read through the replies. I had five.

I dismissed two immediately, as the writers were from the north of the country, and I do not think I can conduct a courtship at such a distance. It has proved difficult enough to establish one in South Kensington. There was a widow from Surrey who knew London well, especially the Notting Hill area, and she had enclosed a photograph. I put the letter to one side, with a 'P' for possible which I pencilled in the top right hand corner.

The fourth letter was so long that I lost the will to read to the end. The lady in question had elected to tell me her life history, and that of her numerous but short-lived relatives. After telling me tales of their education, travels and offspring she would finish off the sentence with 'and then he died', or 'and then she died', depending. I felt I knew the lady well enough without actually having to meet up. In fact I could see you could easily over the course of an evening give up the will to live, and a shapely ankle would be no compensation.

The final letter was from a local lady who seemed keener to find out about my house and income than my humorous personality. Could I reply with accounts, as she had been 'had' that way before. Was the property in my name and did I have any beneficiaries? I felt this was an unsuitable start. Call me old-fashioned, I too am a practical man, and I understand that a woman needs to feel secure, but I think requesting my ledgers a step too far.

I went back to the widow from Surrey and took up the photograph. Oh dear, I am really not at all sure. The pose was very bold. She had one leg up on a chair and her hand was holding up her skirt to reveal her leg (which was shapely) and ankle. Her smile was very knowing and from the angle of the camera it looked as though she was looking straight at me. Very unnerving. I really am starting to think that a dog might suit me better.

—◦◦◦—

The strangest thing happened today. I was clearing up at the end of the day when there was a tap-tap on the door. 'Enter, Mrs Hagley,' I replied, but it was not Rose, it was Jane Wood, the dressmaker from the top floor. I apologized for the error, and asked what I could do to be of service. Mrs Wood apologized too, and said she had not meant to disturb me at the end of the day, but she had a problem which she knew I would be able to help with. It turned out that while changing this evening she had inadvertently stepped on one of her pins, which had gone straight through her shoe, breaking off and leaving the point in her foot. She had tried for the last half hour to remove it, but it was too difficult, and she was concerned that it might cause an infection. Would I be able to help? Of course, I asked her to sit down and take off her slipper. Look as I might I could not see the problem, but was able to reassure her that the offending object was not in evidence. Mrs Wood was graciousness itself, asking at once if she could pay for my time, which I would not hear of. She glanced at my shirt, which had some slight fraying at the cuffs. Would it seem very presumptuous if she offered to 'turn' them for me? Her husband had been hard on his cuffs too, and it was a simple service. I thanked her and said that would be most kind.

I have never spoken more than half a dozen words to Mrs Wood, but there was something about her that evening. She smiled at me in a very engaging way as she left, and I found myself regretting her departure as she quietly walked back up the stairs. I had my supper and thought over the exchange. Could it be that my companion in life is only just on the top landing? She is pretty in a simple, elegant way. Self-contained. I rarely see her, yet from our few words she clearly used to care for the well-being of her husband. I shall take my shirt up (after it has been laundered) and at the same time ask her to accompany me for an evening out. How extraordinary, who would have thought it. Jane — such an unassuming, yet attractive, name.

ROSE HAGLEY

When I took in Mr W.'s post I thought, this won't do. We could have anybody turn up. I didn't tell Arthur, but for some time I have had it in my mind that Mrs Wood would be the ideal wife for Mr W. Whenever we talk I have always thought what a nice woman she is. Kind to the children, asking about Arthur most attentively, and she is clearly a very good seamstress, which is always useful in the home. I left the paper with the advertisement outside her door, drawing a circle around the box, with a question mark beside it. Then I knocked on the door and left. I heard her open her door and pick up the newspaper. A couple of hours later, at the end of the day, she went downstairs, and I heard her talking to Mr W.

Just call me Cupid (Arthur would say stupid). I can't wait to tell Kate.

STUCK BETWEEN FLOORS

In the end, a dog won the day. Albert and Jane did not go off in the sunset together. The decision was a mutual one, not without regret on both sides. Mr Warmbath continued with his practice, and leisure time was taken up in the company of a Lakeland Terrier called Will.

Then came the event which was to shake all in the house (and the world). The coming of the Great War. Mr Warmbath, too old to join up, devoted much time to a paper on the diagnosis of and treatment for trench foot. He also joined The Pedic Clinic in Bloomsbury, where in the evening he could be found offering his services for free to the poor of London.

Arthur Hagley, also too old to enlist, remained at the Talbot factory, where the production of motor cars gave way to that of ambulances. Young Arthur had left Talbot before the start of the war, to better his prospects by working as a mechanic on the London buses. Not long into his new career he found himself driving the very same buses on the Western Front. He had replaced his bus driver's uniform with an army one, and could now be found transporting not commuters, but troops to the front line. He never came home.

Rose Hagley was correct when she thought that the family fate would be tied to the motor industry, just not in a way she could ever have envisioned. Both Rose and her elder daughter went to work as conductors for the London General Omnibus Company. They were, as she put it, 'supporting young Arthur', and she felt closer to him working on the open-topped double decker than at home or in a factory.

After the end of the war, in 1919, Mr Warmbath sells the house and moves to Bloomsbury. The first School of Podiatric Medicine is opened and he is now involved in the teaching of chiropody. This is the most fulfilling period of his career. His knowledge, combined with his humour, makes him an inspiring teacher, and his lectures are filled. The Hagleys, still a troupe, also move on, the house proving too much of a reminder of their loss.

We pick up the fortunes of the house in 1920. No. 53 continues in multiple occupation. An American with the improbable name of Corliss Claflin occupies a suite of three rooms, with his wife, Marnie. They have their own private cooking arrangements, but still share a common bathroom with the other occupants of the house.

Corliss Claflin is the inspiration for this book. His flyer was uncovered stuck in the dust beneath the floorboards during the redecoration of an upstairs room in the year 2000. As the flyer attests, he is running from the house a one-man theatrical, variety and music-hall agency.

THE NEW KEYHOLDERS

SHOW BUSINESS
WINTER 1920

CORLISS CLAFLIN
Aged fifty years, theatrical agent

God, how I love a creative! I am not one, but if you want an audience, applause and a man to appreciate every brushstroke, every page and every entrance, then I am that man. Maybe it is the American within. We were born to cheer and I am a cheerleader. This is an underrated talent. Every artist needs affirmation, but few can give it with feeling. I am the master of affirmation. Feeling a touch of writer's block? – Call me in. Worried you haven't found the psychology behind a character? – Call me in.

This doesn't mean I am a vapid individual. I just understand that inner need to be loved. My career path had not been obvious, but I really do feel that I have found my niche at last. I am happy to be termed a 'late developer' (eleventh hour, in truth).

I was born in Chicago, and God, how I loved it. Wealth, squalor, people, a buzzing, heaving mass of life. A city to be young in. There was not a hotel, theatre or dive that I didn't visit, and the women . . . Sadly, my lifestyle was a cause of some pain to my father. There was an unfortunate incident when I was linked to the socialite Gloria Taylor, such a heavenly woman, but regrettably already taken. The *Chicago Tribune* printed a photograph of us leaving a restaurant, underneath the headline 'The Poor Taste Café' and that was that: my lifestyle apparently was not enhancing the family name.

I was somewhat surprised by this intervention. My father being no slouch when it came to the seduction of younger woman. A doctor, with a side interest in spiritualism, he warmly suggested that I take myself across the pond and see life elsewhere, from a different perspective.

The decision was taken to remove me from that city of happiness and send me to reside with my fabulous aunt, Tennessee Claflin, who by some extraordinary quirk of fate had managed to tie the knot with an English lord – Sir Francis Cook, Viscount of Montserrat (another man interested in the life beyond, his dead wife having conveniently risen to pronounce her approval). My new home, London, was considered a safe and salubrious option. I was provided with a small stipend, deemed enough for me to live on, but not enough to indulge the more amusing aspects of my social life.

Not one to dwell on the unhappiness in life, I got off the boat, and found myself lodging in some splendour in the Richmond area. Doughty House was my aunt's London abode, up on the hill overlooking the river Thames. Auntie Tennie C. (oh dear, how she hated to be called that) was abroad when I arrived, but she had left me an introduction to the watercolour artist William Stockdale, who was also visiting. He proved a kindly old gentleman of seventy-six, more interested in gardening than in his young wife, Sophia, a delightful creature, a mere thirty-six, who was keen to be my guide about town.

I have always thought that to be really involved in the arts you need to participate fully, throw yourself in hook and line. It gives you the authority to move among those rare beings and gain an acceptance that might otherwise be lacking. And I have always had a particular interest in the mindset of writers. So, I decided to set up my stall as a book publisher. With Sophia's help and connections, I could see myself discovering the next Dickens or trading *mots justes* with the Bloomsburys, but let's cut to the chase – shall we just say I was not well suited to the book trade. Too many words.

I realized about the same time that life had become a little too cosy, living as I was in a rather surprising *ménage à trois*. God, it was fun. But I had to move on when it became clear that Sophia was forming too strong an attachment. I did not want to be the cause of a break-up in the happy home – or, worse, see thunder clouds rolling into William's bucolic scenes.

I was pondering on my next move, when, as is often the case, Fate took a hand. I was strolling up the Strand, wondering whether to take in a cocktail at the Savoy and see where the day took me, when I passed by a small sign in the window of an office block: 'Photographer's studio to rent'. Immediately I realized that this was my vocation.

I knew I had not got the technical expertise to wield the camera myself, but I was sure I could hire an assistant for the practical (and, to my mind, rather dull) side of the business, while I would provide the front of house, so to speak. Without wasting a moment I went in, and so it was that by the time I eventually reached the Savoy I was the proprietor of a small central London photographic studio. I also had in my pocket a calling card from the previous owner, who, while unable to meet the overheads for his business, possessed the know-how and, more importantly, the equipment necessary for my new adventure.

Corliss Claflin, portrait photographer. My God, how I loved it.

My accent was a huge selling point, giving the studio a glamour that the block itself rather lacked. It was soon clear why the previous owner had fallen out of favour. Although a whizz when it came to focus, he had no idea how to soothe and cajole the customer. I spent some of my new earnings on sets and costumes, and could soon create the impression of a tropical island paradise or a Wild West saloon, with my subjects suitably suited and booted, while encouraged to strike poses with attitude. My canteen was the Savoy, the bar a joy to frequent, and usually my bill covered by new clients that I met over cocktails. Sharing the office block was a theatrical agent. Soon I had built up quite a reputation, taking portraits of the talent that came through his doors.

I have to say it was all going rather well. I was living in digs in Rostrevor Road, Fulham. The widowed landlady, a dear soul, saw to my every need. Then came the war.

My photography ambitions proceeded to take a somewhat different turn. My assistant had joined up in the first wave. I was sorry to see him go, but by that time I had become quite proficient. I decided to remain in London for the duration. I was too old to actively participate anyway, and there was nothing for me in Chicago. I began taking photos of the home front, which I sold into various publications. Women at work, that sort of thing. (Please God, save me from ever having to see another factory floor. Assembly lines don't do it for me, however lovely the women.)

I managed to maintain my studio, where my main source of business was now family snapshots to be sent to husbands, sons and sweethearts at the Front. So many images — I must have taken hundreds, the island set being replaced by a rather homespun room to remind the boys that a warm hearth waited back at home. My personal contribution to the propaganda of war. How many died with those memories crushed in their jackets? I don't propose to dwell on it.

The Savoy miraculously survived unscathed and was a haven from the life in khaki going on outside. I am not good with gloom.

It was during this time that I met the woman who was to become my wife. Not just my wife, my pal.

MARNIE CLAFLIN
Aged forty-six years
Wife to CORLISS

'Marnie Macdonald, will you be my pal?'

I thought and still think that those are the most romantic words anyone has ever said to me. Corliss makes me feel attractive, amusing and loved. Actually, he does that to all women, he is an incorrigible flirt, but nobody else is or — I hope — will be his 'pal'. I don't think I have ever heard the word applied to another woman. 'Pals' are men. It is also so deliciously American — the British have 'chums', which doesn't resonate during the process of seduction — 'pal' is a word that needs to be spoken with an American accent. When Corliss comes home he doesn't say 'Hello' or 'Good evening' – he calls up, 'Where's my pal?'

I met him going into the *Daily Mirror*. He was delivering some photographs for a feature on the 'fight for the Englishman's home', I was going up to the editor's office, where I worked three days a week as a secretary (the other four spent volunteering for the war effort). By the time we were passing the picture desk I had somehow agreed to accompany him to a show at the Savoy Theatre.

We were lucky to get tickets (well, it wasn't really luck, Corliss took the manager to one side as we entered). It was not an entirely suitable play for a first date, rather brutal and intense, starring Harry Irving. Our seats were certainly not the best (the side, first row, giving us an excellent view up the actor's trouser legs – I could also smell his sweat). So, while not the most relaxing of shows, it certainly gave us something to discuss over supper. I told Corliss I had never seen such moving ankles, and that I was certain, had I seen his face, there would have been tears. Of course, Corliss loved the show. He is a fan of high drama whatever the angle.

It seems like we have been together a lifetime, though in reality it is only four years. Since that first meeting, the war has ended, we have married, moved and Corliss is establishing his new career. Put like that it all seems faintly ridiculous. Life condensed. We are not young, neither of us was actively looking for love – or, indeed, lust – but I think it is rare to find a 'pal', the person that you are happy just to be with. It is extraordinary that neither of us had married before, but I am not the sort of woman who feels inadequate without a man at her side. I don't need a husband, or I didn't until now. I can't see children coming our way either. Neither of us is really bothered by this (Corliss says he would be a 'hopeless father', which may be true – there is something of the child in him), but I do have a small regret that I won't see him interact with small Claflins.

We have moved into lodgings (Corliss likes to call them our 'digs') in Earl's Court. Two rooms, with a kitchen in between, on the top floor. One room will be our office. I am to be working alongside. I could never have imagined that I would be (what does Corliss call it ?) 'schmoozing' theatricals.

CORLISS CLAFLIN

In my entire life I could count on one hand the people you meet who actually make you feel better for the encounter, and I have met a lot of people. The ones you can get drunk with, the ones you can laugh with, even the ones you can cry with, these guys are two a penny.

This other thing has nothing to do with humour, or warmth, or compassion, and you absolutely can't fake it. As I walked up the stairs the first day I met Marnie, I knew she had it. I was feeling better by the minute for having met her. It wasn't what she said, it was probably what she didn't. Marnie isn't soppy, she's sharp as a tack, but when she looks at you and smiles she is absolutely, totally engaged. There is never a feeling that she would like to move off elsewhere. Every bit of babble, even from the biggest bores, is treated by her with a humour and interest that I tell her they could not possibly deserve. Age doesn't phase her, or social class. Marnie won't go into a room and jockey for position, she just enjoys every encounter.

God, I know I talk too much, and by the time we had reached our respective offices, she knew pretty much everything about me and I knew nothing about her. But I had managed to secure her company for the evening. We have been together ever since.

As the war ended there was one thing I knew, I had 'done' photography. During the time at my studio I had made friends with the theatrical agent across the corridor. A fine fellow, with a very respectable stable of talent. I had spent spare time studying the form. I have always loved the theatre, good or bad. Indeed, as I said to Marnie, it is in the blood. Aunt Tennessee used to perform in her youth as 'The Wonderful Child', falling into trances and hearing voices — rumour went about *en famille* that she had prophesied the death of Abraham Lincoln. God, what a woman! It was all so obvious. I decided to set up my own theatrical agency. The only mystery was why it had not occurred to me before.

I have rented three rooms near Earl's Court underground station, and organized the printing of flyers. I am a sucker when it comes to a smart address and felt mentioning 'South Kensington' as our location would give the business a cachet it might otherwise lack. We are only a short hop away, so barely misleading. As I unpacked the new stationery, it was with some irritation I noted the printers had misspelt the name of the road. Marnie had already pointed out that she felt they had sold their services too cheap, and by the time I attempted to return the boxes, the shop had shut — permanently. Well, if that is to be our only setback, I can live with it.

Finsborough Road it is — what's in a name?

MARNIE CLAFLIN

Corliss is such an enthusiast. Stationery cements a business, there it is for all to see. Up to that point it is words in the ether.

When Corliss showed me the shop in the Earl's Court Road, I could see it already had the air of a company that had seen better times. He had, of course, already committed to the order, so there was little to be done but cross our fingers. Invoice books, headed paper, a large ledger and flyers had all been signed off, and at this point we had not found a single artist. Corliss said it would concentrate the mind, equipping the 'office' was integral to the launch, and he pointed out it wasn't just actors who needed to 'feel the part'.

He seemed to think that 'talent' was easily found, and indeed he had already started placing small advertisements in *The Stage* and *The Era*, stating that our 'books are always open' and specifying that we could 'always place acts of quality'. 'The bigger the turn the better we like it.' 'Small turns given utmost consideration.' There were more variations on this theme and, indeed, letters were starting to come in. Corliss was absolutely thrilled with the new stationery. In fact, he brought it home in a cab. As I opened the first pack, I was of two minds whether to mention the error or just leave it. I was loath to cast an air of gloom on the inaugural day. Corliss didn't notice it at all at first, he just kept marvelling as he placed the paper in piles on the shelves. It was when he decided to sign his name on the opening page of the ledger that he spotted the mistake. Far from sinking into gloom, he repacked everything and carted the whole lot back to Earl's Court.

We had been their final commission. I honestly think the 'closed' sign was slapped on the door as he left the premises. Back came the boxes. Corliss said, 'What's in a name? Finborough? Finsborough? Most people can't read anyway.' It turns out he was right. I think since we have been going only one person has ever pointed out the discrepancy. Theatricals, it seems, only look at the elements of a contract pertinent to them; once past their name and the wage they drift off, our address an item of little or no interest.

Corliss put up some of his theatrical portraits around the walls. I had bought a small palm that I placed in a china urn in the corner, and we celebrated with an absolutely disgusting concoction that Corliss assured me was 'just the thing at the Savoy'. Apparently it is called a 'Hanky Panky', the chief pleasure being the glass and a piece of orange that he had placed artistically on the top.

The only way to drink it was in one go, and then we had another, followed by another, by which time an 's' here or there was of little concern to either of us. We spent the evening at the Shepherd's Bush Empire, which we both decided was a work-related outing, although I have to confess that the Hanky Pankys had taken their toll. I dozed off on Corliss's shoulder only to be woken by the sound of applause, so you could say that the launch was not entirely auspicious. Day two I had a bad head, but I could smell the coffee and see Corliss through the kitchen door wearing my robe and humming the tune to 'The daring young man on the flying trapeze'. I got up, wrapped the sheet around me and joined in the chorus — 'His movements were graceful, all girls he could please, and my love he has stolen away.' Not a bad start to a new business.

CORLISS CLAFLIN

English, American and Continental. I said to Marnie, let's put out the appeal to all points. After all, I am American, I live here and, God, I love abroad. Equally, I don't like to specialize. I don't want to end up with a list of ageing thespians or finding myself locked into comedic turns. They are always such gloomy individuals when not performing. One or two I can cope with. All comers, that's the way. The best of all worlds.

We are 'Corliss Claflin & Co.', Marnie being the Co. The small ads are paying off. We have had about twenty replies from the first week. Marnie is tasked with sifting through them, and then I can do the meet up — by appointment only. I don't want to find them loitering on the doorstep. In the meantime I have been writing copious letters to theatre managers introducing myself. I intend to go on a charm offensive round town as soon as we have signed up our initial artists. I suppose the provinces will be our bread and butter, and I may have to catch a train or two, let's see. I am not good with small town dynamics. My older brother, Albert, is the reverse. He is, of all things, a sewing machine salesman. He has spent his entire life on the road, selling hemstitch and bobbins to sad housewives who live in the middle of nowhere, USA. Every year we get another Christmas card from an address more bizarre than the last. I have experienced small town life through those cards, and I cannot say it appeals.

First things first. I have been put up for membership of the Garrick. It is important to be seen with the movers, and if there is one thing I do well it is to bring a touch of bonhomie to the party. I told Marnie, forget the Hanky Panky, I intend to find out the secret behind the Garrick Club Punch, which I believe involves a hint of maraschino liqueur. She said she would have the glasses polished and at the ready.

God, what a girl!

MARNIE CLAFLIN

Corliss has left me to look through the list of would-bes. The one thing they all share is dissatisfaction with their previous agent, no surprise there. Some are already in work, touring the provinces, which will send Corliss into a flat spin. I cannot seeing him boarding the train to Peterborough or wherever. But maybe he will surprise me. I shall set up appointments from my shortlist, and we can take it from there. There is quite a selection, some with more experience than others.

A couple of child acts have written in. I know they are popular. They make both Corliss and me feel rather sick, but that is not the point. I have asked the Baby Canary and her mother to come over this Wednesday morning and Rudy Ronaldo and his mother in the afternoon. Apparently, Rudy is known for his ball manipulation and can juggle hats and cocktail shakers, so he will be right up Corliss's street. I thought we could finish off the afternoon with a dog act, so I have Miss Jenny and Fifi in for 4 o'clock. I feel like quite the impresario.

Oh, dear. Corliss not as excited as I had hoped. He said, 'Oh God, children and animals – on the same day? Do you want to kill me?' I told him to shut up, and hold judgement until he had seen them. He just laughed and said he had booked seats for a show at the Chelsea Palace and after we could go to the Ritz for Bloody Marys. He said that might give him the strength he would need for Wednesday. I said, 'Remember your aunt – you told me she drove them wild in the aisles.' He replied, 'Yes, in 1858.' He could see I was looking a bit crestfallen, so he said sorry, and that he was only joking, and he was much looking forward to all of them, especially Fifi. Could we change and go now? He didn't want to miss the overture, and Mabel Thorne, the comedienne, was first up. We decided to walk, as I had been in the house all day. I felt quite fired up after the performances, and absolutely cheered up after the Ritz.

Are we going to make any money?

CORLISS CLAFLIN

Such a good evening. I told Marnie I wanted to hold on to the memories. With this in mind I begged her to start the interviews without me, promising to return well in time for Fifi. It is not important for me to attend to the minutiae. I assured her that my time would be well spent. I intend to go back to the Chelsea Palace Theatre and leave my card for Mr Berlin the manager, and then I need to visit my aunt in Richmond.

I have not spoken to Aunt Tennessee for some weeks, and I am keen to keep her up to speed with the new venture. Although she is getting quite an age, I'm delighted to say she is still firing on all cylinders, loves to hear the gossip from town, and is always good for a glass of something interesting . She has been supportive of my ventures both in spirit and coin over the years. As she's a woman who reinvents herself every time the sun comes up, I can absolutely say that she 'gets me'.

My other aunt, Victoria, is a riot too, but at present resides in Worcestershire. She encountered her third husband, John

Biddulph Martin, at one of her London lectures. Sadly, he gave up the will in 1901. She is now engaged in a scheme to educate the village youth by modernizing the kindergarten classes. This is rich. As far as I recall she had little formal education herself. Never mind she was considered so disreputable that William Vanderbilt coughed up the cash for her passage to England, with small change left over for the essentials. As I say, it's in the blood.

Anyway, Worcestershire is absolutely not on my beat. We occasionally exchange letters, hers being of a more challenging nature than mine. She enjoys a robust debate, which you might expect from someone who put herself up for president of the US at thirty-five. I find there are few subjects on which she does not hold an opinion. I attended a lecture she gave on abortion and eugenics. One was quite enough, but at least I showed willing.

The two aunts have spent a lifetime causing riot and mayhem on both sides of the Atlantic, and have been a strong influence in my life. They are one of the many reasons that I adore the fairer sex. They are both absolutely mad, and all the better for it.

Marnie protested about being left on her own for the interviews, saying she knew 'nothing about engaging acts'. What's there to know, I said, just see if you like them. That's half the battle, if you like them so will an audience. There was still an hour before the Singing Canary whistled her way in, so we spent half of it in the bedroom and then I swiftly exited the house to give her ample time to prepare for the day's excitements.

God, I love this job. I bumped into the postman as I was leaving, and took another bundle of letters off his hands. I left them on the hall stairs to retrieve at a later hour. I had just reached the end of the road when I could swear I spotted the Canary child, complete with mother, coming towards me. Marnie is in for a treat.

MARNIE CLAFLIN

Too unfair. I have never met either of Corliss's notorious aunts and I could see his day was panning out better than mine. Anyway, it is all a novelty, and having tidied myself and the room up I had five minutes to practise sitting behind our desk, before I heard the bell downstairs. I peered over the top of the banisters and heard the maid opening the door, and instructing the visitors to proceed to the top. I adjusted my smile and waited.

The morning began to turn into something rather surreal. The Baby Canary was called Annie, and looked somewhat older than the promised seven years. Her mother, Mrs Martha Gray, heaved up the stairs a large bag which she placed between them, as they sat opposite me, looking expectant.

I could see that they were more used to the process than I. Mrs Gray smiled tightly, and asked when Mr Claflin would be appearing. I explained that it was just me, Mr Claflin being otherwise engaged organizing the setting up of a revue in Chelsea. She looked around the room, and enquired which of the artists in the photographs were on our books. I said all of them, which may have stretched a point, as Corliss had boosted his collection with pictures of Buster Keaton and Myrna Loy. 'Some are on our American books,' I added, desperately. Mrs Gray raised her eyebrows and continued to scan the room.

In an attempt to gain control of the situation, I asked if Annie would be prepared to give me a sample of her act.

It was as though I had opened a jack-in-the-box. Annie sprang up and flung off her coat to reveal a slightly grubby yellow dress. Although the costume had seen better days, Annie fluffed up the ruffles before delving into the copious bag to produce a ukulele. Then, with a toss of her curls and a suggestive wiggle, she gave voice to a rollicking version of 'Yes, sir, that's my baby', finishing off with a few tap steps and kisses to the audience – me.

I sat, stunned. Mrs Gray's face was a study in smug satisfaction. Annie packed up her uke, replaced her coat and sat neatly back on her chair, clearly waiting for a response.

The only thing going through my mind was where was Corliss when you need him. We ran through the particulars, address, previous work and current agent. Mrs Gray gave me a photograph of Annie and a list of her commitments over the next couple of months. Actually I was quite impressed, she had more work in her diary than we had (well, not difficult). I told them we would be in touch, and that Annie was a little treasure, which seemed to cheer them both up. Mrs Gray said that she would look forward to a proposal, and they were not afraid of travel. We parted on friendly terms and as I saw them out I noticed a pile of letters addressed to the agency sitting on the bottom of the stairs. 'We can't keep up,' I said to Mrs Gray, gesturing to the post, as they left. I started sifting through them as I went back upstairs.

Where is Corliss? I need to get better at this.

CORLISS CLAFLIN

It is all going better than I could possibly have imagined. When I arrived at the Chelsea Palace, I was delighted to find an acquaintance from my photographic days in the foyer – an actor who, while never going to be cast in the lead role, nevertheless keeps at it. Rarely out of work, he is a solid player, a character actor, popular with his peers and the public. I had done some head shots for him, after which we had ventured out to the Savoy and spent a most amusing evening together. He was in rehearsal for an up-and-coming show, and offered to introduce me to Mr Berlin, who turned out to be an individual of charm and intelligence. We all repaired to a local public house, where it was agreed that my new agency was a fine thing, and Mr Berlin said as soon as I had completed my signings he wished to hear from me immediately. They still had spaces for the coming season, and he could see that recognizing talent would be second nature to me. My pal will be thrilled. Marnie has been worrying needlessly about our finances. My instinct was correct. I am better when freed from the yoke.

I bade a convivial farewell to my companions and headed to Richmond, where Aunt Tennie C. was taking a nap. I passed an hour with a walk by the river, and then headed back for tea and refreshments. The time flew by, and I noticed with horror that it was well past four o'clock, and I knew that Fifi would have been walked several times around the block by the time I returned.

I was pressed to stay for an early supper, which I did. I see so little of the old dear, and thought I should make the most of it. My God, she was on good form. We talked free love, suffragettes and banking. Now, that's a woman. As I was leaving she insisted on giving me a cheque to help with starting costs, saying she expected front row seats for any new openings. Well, I was safe in that promise as she can barely get beyond the front door. I took a cab home.

'Where's my pal?', I called as I came in. Marnie was asleep, her head on the desk surrounded by letters and photographs from artistes who were clearly fighting to join our books.

I kissed the top of her head and helped her to our bedroom, where she started to tell me about her day. I put a finger to her lips. There is a time for work.

MARNIE CLAFLIN

Well, I must say I feel like I have spent several lives in show business. Acts good, bad and just plain extraordinary have been up and down our stairs in the past few weeks. I have seen singers, dancers, jugglers, magic acts and comics – and that is just the start.

I find comics the hardest to watch. There is something strange about hearing jokes (especially old jokes) told across the desk. A laugh seems out of place, a smile not quite enough and no reaction at all an insult. I was not expecting to audition them as such, but all seem keen to showcase their talents and it seems I am better than no audience at all. Interestingly, they are all very punctual and keen to engage, and all have a tale to tell. In truth, sometimes it is impossible to get them out of the door once they have settled in. I told Corliss, who said, 'God, my poor angel — just give me a quick curtain any day', and smiled. I was not sure if this was some sort of *double entendre* (the comics are getting to me), so decided to ignore him.

I have improved my technique enormously. In fact, the interviews are now second nature to me. I can read through a letter and tell straight away if it is worth asking them to come in. I have signed about ten acts. Some are starting immediately, others have obligations to fulfil before they can join us. I decided against the Baby Canary, but we have Rudy Ronaldo and Fifi on the books.

Rudy is a charming boy of about fourteen. He actually came without any of his props, but I offered up our cocktail shaker, a couple of hats and two golf balls that I found in the desk drawer (where *had* they come from?). Well, I was so impressed that I actually clapped. His mother said he had started with the dinner knives as a harmless way of relieving stress. I had a go with the golf balls, not successful, but it made for a friendly atmosphere. I said I would send out our standard contract and proposals and would wait to hear from them. Mr Ronaldo senior apparently went back to Italy before the war, and although they receive postcards from the Naples area every couple of months, the man himself has proved elusive. I found myself offering helpful advice. This is what I mean by tales. I must not encourage them to talk about their personal lives. I am sure it affects my judgement. They replied by return and Rudy was our first signing.

Fifi is a French poodle (I waited as long as I could for Corliss, but there came a point). Jenny, her trainer, used to work with a terrier called Topper. Sadly, Topper passed away, and having another terrier was too traumatic, every day a painful reminder of tricks gone by – hence, a poodle. Fifi is brilliant at riding a bicycle, and can count. Both have a variety of matching costumes, indeed they both turned up in charming cocktail hats. Jenny comes from a family of circus entertainers, but both prefer vaudeville, as life on the road takes its toll, apparently. I did point out that they will still have to travel – no problem there, a rooming house preferable to a caravan any day. I nodded sagely, as though I were never out of a wagon. Jenny said Fifi also has a phobia about clowns. I too find clowns unnerving, and never at all funny, so I could honestly reply I knew just how she felt. Of course, she is just as likely to encounter clowns in the theatre, but we will cross that bridge when and if. More tales.

It has fallen on me to find our clients. I should have known that the first day. When Corliss came home I was dozing at the desk. My first twelve hours had been quite challenging, so I was keen to fill him in on the events. He said I had done quite enough, and he looked forward to hearing all about it in the morning. He said he had sorted out our finances for the next couple of months, so I should take it easy.

I must say, I slept incredibly well. When I woke up, Corliss was already dressed and seemed about to leave the house. 'Where are you off to?' I said. He came back into the room. 'I am off to recce the Fulham Theatre, and then I may walk on down to Shepherd's Bush. I was leaving you a note. Will you be all right? I see you have everything under control here. What a girl! Where shall we dine tonight? Let's decide later. God, how I love and adore you – no one else could possibly look so heavenly first thing in the morning.'

He kissed my toes, which were sticking out from the blanket, and left with a smile and a wave. I heard him disappearing down the stairs, and the door opening. He called up the stairs as he left, 'More letters! Can you believe it?'

And the door closed.

CORLISS CLAFLIN

Delegation, that is the route to a successful business. Understand your key strengths and stick to them. Marnie is therapist, travel agent and talent scout all rolled into one glorious package. I would be hopeless at the interviews, and basic practicalities. Who would have thought they would expect their travel arrangements to be taken care of? Can't these people do anything for themselves? If there is the slightest change they fall about in a complete state and letters come flying to and fro. I haven't Marnie's patience. That woman is simply a saint. We have signed up about fifteen artistes at the last count up (could be more by now, I can just about keep track). My pal sits me down and goes through all the photographs, fills me in on their background, what they do and where they have performed. Finally, I am tasked with getting them placed.

I have been forced on board a couple of trains, but I have to say I rather enjoyed my days out. I had the pleasure to bump into Oswald Stoll at the Garrick, and he insisted on me accompanying him to Bristol to see the Hippodrome. What a theatre! Glamour oozes from every corner and it holds nearly two thousand people. The dome apparently slides back, opening the auditorium up to the stars and sky. God, I adored it! On the train home we discussed my agency, and I told him how I had been down at the Empire Shepherd's Bush only the day before. We left firm friends. For God's sake, the man owns at least ten variety theatres. He loves the Savoy as much as I do, and is going to make sure I have all the relevant details for the various managers. We are peas in a pod, both agreeing that business should always be a pleasure. 'Luxury' and 'sumptuous entertainment' are words that kept cropping up. A man so totally after my own heart. During the journey Oswald suggested that I use the talent we have on the books and put together a revue to present to the managers. Great idea, and one I had already been considering. Ship them all out in one go, what could be better?

We have (apparently) a delicious row of girl dancers (where was I for that one?), who not only kick up a storm but sing in four-part harmony, and a sensational balancing act who perform dressed as bears; add to that the comedy jazz band and Madame Zozo and I should say we have an evening to remember − and that's before I even bring Fifi into the equation! Let's call it *Starry Nights*.

God, I'm on form.

MARNIE CLAFLIN

I must say, I have never seen Corliss so cheerful, and that is saying something. To be honest, at the moment I hardly see him at all, but when I do he is filled with an enthusiasm that is very endearing. His days (and nights) are spent in a whirl of wining and dining. There is not a producer, manager or impresario that he doesn't seem to know. Often he doesn't get home until the early hours of the morning. There is always some group or other going on at the end of a show. I can't keep up. I have tried to join him a couple of times in the week, but I simply don't have the stamina. We seem to be working shifts. I do worry about his health. I can't tell him, but he's not young any more. He is carrying on the life style of a twenty-year-old. He chain-smokes cigars, and any profit we do make he spends in the bar. The other morning I heard him with an appalling cough, which he laughed off, saying he was only attempting to gain my attention.

I have to admit the socializing is paying off. He has a knack of convincing everybody that he is on to the new next thing. He radiates confidence. We (I) have signed twenty-six acts at the last count, and I am working round the clock on administration and logistics. Corliss has rather brilliantly taken to sorting them into groups and presenting them to producers as a revue − *Starry Nights* is playing in Bournemouth, off to Lyme Regis tomorrow, *Light up the Night* has just opened in Bath, while Rudy and Fifi are supporting acts in Shepherd's Bush, The rest of our crew is scattered around the country, working the halls. Organized chaos. We have been forced to negotiate rates, but it has meant that we are keeping everyone on the move and employed. Sometimes I think I should have shares in the railways, the amount of time the acts spend on the train.

Corliss has found me an assistant. A young ASM, who needs to earn extra money and is free four mornings a week. His name is Karl and he has proved a gem. It is blissful to have someone to share the day with, and he understands the world so well that I sometimes wonder who is employing who. His parents work in the theatre and he has grown up backstage. Nothing phases him – in fact he relishes a panic, which is lucky, as there is always something. I think life would change if we had a telephone. Karl is going to look into it. At the present time he can be found sorting out the dramas at Earl's Court underground station, where they have installed a telephone box. I keep in a supply of pennies, so at least he can get through to the theatres when disaster strikes.

While Corliss spends our money on drinks, I seem to spend it on telegrams.

Which reminds me, Corliss has just received one from his Aunt Tennessee. Just a one-liner: 'COME NOW.' Straight to the point.

CORLISS CLAFLIN

I must say, Aunt T. chooses her moments. I am up to my neck with the shows, I have engagements spanning out over the next couple of weeks, and to be truthful I am not feeling the best. My pal says I have to cut down on the dining, but it really is key to finding out the who, what and where in the entertainment world. I sent a telegram back saying 'NOTED. CAN WE SAY FRIDAY WEEK?' I received a reply by return – 'FRIDAY WEEK? I SAID NOW.'

Really, that woman is too demanding. I shall have to book out this Thursday and devote the day to the project. Once you have got to Richmond I find there is not much time left for anything else. No matter. I have not had a dinner *à deux* with Marnie for ages, so I will pencil her in for a late supper. She will be agog to find out what is so urgent that it requires me to drop all. We could go to the Café Royal, we love that dining room. Maybe dancing afterwards.

A night on the town with my pal. Heaven.

MARNIE CLAFLIN

What's wrong with a coddled egg in bed? Corliss seems to have forgotten what it is like to eat at home. I might as well turn the kitchen over to filing cabinets for all the use we get from it.

Apparently Corliss likes to know that it is there, 'just in case'. In case the Criterion burns down, I suppose. He is there today. One of his lunch clubs is meeting up — I think they have a guest speaker.

Still it will be nice to get out, and get dressed up, I seem to live in the same old, same old. Not much point getting dolled up to move from one room to another.

What can his aunt want? We speculated this morning. Corliss is hopeful that she is going to announce that she intends to leave her fortune to C. Claflin. Hmmmm. Although she has been generous to her favourite nephew over the years, she is not stupid. Corliss protested, saying, 'Come awn, I'm good with money.' Well, I suppose it depends how you look at it. I would replace 'good' with 'generous' — which is a positive characteristic. But he is not one to put a bit on hold for a rainy day.

Talking of which, getting the fees out of the various managements is a nightmare. If it were practical I would wait outside their offices and collect the cheques personally, but it's not. Karl is better than me. After we have sent out the standard reminders, he's off to the box in Earl's Court and stays on the line until he gets through to accounts. It's all down to a man's voice. I talk tough, but they don't believe me. Corliss doesn't want to get involved. He says they wouldn't believe him either, and that Karl is our bare-knuckle street fighter (a bad analogy as there is not a muscle on him).

As soon as the money comes in, it goes out. I can't bear to keep the talent waiting. Karl (again!) says we shouldn't pay everyone straight away, but keep them on hold or stagger the payments. I said, 'You would have Fifi waiting by the bowl for her biscuits?' He replied, 'Yes, absolutely I would. If the money could remain in your account for just for a few days, I would see it as repayment for my efforts. It is the way of the world, Marnie, and will help build up your credit.'

Genius, but he doesn't have to listen to the tales. In fact, he really doesn't. If he is in the room when one or other of our clients appears, he sighs and rolls his eyes as soon as they start off. Karl says it comes with the territory and if I did a spell in stage management even I would become hardened to their moaning. I'm sure he's right. But no biscuits for Fifi? That boy has no heart.

CORLISS CLAFLIN

The great thing about relatives is they have an ability to come at you from left field. I could not think what it was that Tennie wished to impart. Money sprang to my mind. There is a tendency among my older friends (the ones still in funds) to worry about the details of inheritance. I said to my pal (fingers crossed and keep a bottle on ice for later), Tennie has no children, and I have been a dutiful nephew.

When the Viscount shuffled off the mortal coil (many years back), the title went to his son by an earlier marriage, but he still left a large chunk to Auntie for her various needs, and she has remained ensconced in the family home. There was a moment after his death that she decided to have a go at banking, not in any practical sense, but she liked the idea of actually owning one. It was a short-lived enterprise and soon closed its doors, leaving behind a few disgruntled investors. But finance has remained at the forefront of her mind, and she shows lively interest in the goings-on in the City.

Anyways, I arrived punctually at 12.20 p.m. to be shown into the drawing room. There was no preamble. Aunt T. was sitting on the chaise longue surrounded by large vellum scrapbooks, filled with page after page of newspaper articles, photographs and poster clippings. I accepted a glass from Fred, the aged factotum who has been devoted to her cause since the invention of the tray, and sat down.

She gestured at the books. 'Now, see here, Corliss, it simply will not do.' I looked at her quizzically. 'Look, boy, look.' And she stabbed at the pages again. I took one up and began to study the articles. There were some racy photos of Aunt Vi and some really excellent headlines: 'Victoria Woodhull arrested for Obscenity'; 'Victoria Woodhull supports legalization of sex workers'; 'Victoria the Bewitching Broker'. I settled down to enjoy the read. Some of the pieces were new to me, but over the years I have heard most of the gossip that surrounded the two of them. The more salacious stories have become my party piece (some of the tales are so shocking that even I could not embellish them).

'Yes?' I said, mildly. 'These seem to tell it how it is, Auntie Tennie.'

I was treated to one of her looks.

'No, Corliss, that is my problem. They seem to "tell it", as you put it, from one point of view only. Where am I in all of this?'

Her arm swept dramatically over the pile of papers.

'I will tell you. I am here.'

She picked up a small, slim volume and waved it before me.

God. The bottom line is that Aunt Tennessee is jealous of her older sister.

I was treated to a diatribe on the subject, backed up by the articles, and it was true that all the pieces seemed to focus primarily on Victoria. Tennie was keen to point out that, far from lagging behind, she had been the front-runner.

'Did Cornelius Vanderbilt love Victoria? No, Corliss, he did not. Did your grandfather bill Victoria as "The Wonderful Child"? No, Corliss, he did not. Did Victoria marry a viscount? No, Corliss, she did not.'

This conversation was starting to remind me of a music hall act. I glanced at Fred, wondering if he was going to join in, but he was looking straight ahead, tray at the ready. The list of grievances grew apace.

'Victoria has made much of the fact she ran for President (getting nowhere, I may add), but I, Corliss, ran for Congress – and I was considered by all the greater beauty. Indeed, we would never have gone to jail, had it not been for Victoria. All this needs to be addressed, and addressed before I die, and you will be the one to address it.'

Oh, God.

MARNIE CLAFLIN

Corliss returned home after his visit in a cab, with about a dozen huge volumes of newspaper cuttings and a present of a small but exquisite blue and white Chinese ginger jar. I cheerily enquired if it contained Auntie T's ashes, the response being a sardonic 'nearly'. I put the jar on the mantelpiece in the bedroom, where It looked quite at home. I popped in and out to look at it as we carried the books into the office, leaving them on the floor in a corner, our shelves either too narrow or too full to hold them.

Corliss has received his instructions. In a nutshell, his aunt expects him to redress the balance. She has been told by her doctors that she is ill, and should think about putting her affairs in order. Looking back on her life, she sees that her older sister has taken centre stage. And she feels hard done by. She is prepared to leave a portion of her estate to help Corliss with his future (you would think he was twenty), and in return expects him to use his connections in the arts to get her back in the headlines. Far from wanting to hide from her scandals, she wishes them exposed.

Auntie T. is not too bothered, it seems, how he does this. A series of lectures, an exhibition – even a musical was mooted, with Jerome Kern and 'that nice Mr Wodehouse' apparently mentioned as writers. The key to the whole venture is to be the subject matter: 'It must be all about *me*.' Victoria apparently can be included, but very much in a rather dull supporting role. I was stunned. I had always been led to believe that the sisters were joined at the hip.

I asked Corliss if Aunt V. was aware of Aunt T.'s feelings. He thought not, pointing out that they are both so entirely self-centred, it would not have come up in any conversation they were likely to have. 'Will you mention it?' I enquired. 'Oh God, absolutely not,' was the reply.

Corliss said he had had enough of family for one day, and not to forget he had reserved a table at the Café Royal, where we could talk on any subject apart from his aunts. Please would I tell him about my day, and had *Starry Nights* made it to Lyme Regis? I told him that was last week, and, as far as I could recollect, Madame Zozo was now charming Bridport. We left the house in high spirits, humming tunes and making up lyrics about his aunt. It's astonishing how many words you can rhyme with Tennessee when you put your mind to it.

CORLISS CLAFLIN

Well, as it's all down to me, I am going with the musical option. I am trying to persuade Oswald to come in on the venture. This is something really to get my teeth into. I have been staring the idea in the face (so to speak) for years. I really am a shockingly late developer. Auntie T. has already started to fund the project, saying that I cannot possibly do all the work from a top floor room in a lodging house. Apparently, I must have space and I must have a proper home that suits my career. She is proposing to buy us a house, maybe slightly nearer to Richmond. Marnie is looking at properties near Putney and is happy to do the spade work as long as I promise her a telephone.

Tennie is really not well, in fact I am doubtful she will see the project out, so I shall not be saying anything to Auntie V. on the subject. In fact I can see no good reason to mention it until we call 'Overture and Beginners' and the lights fade. I am not one to cause disharmony.

My pal has convinced Karl that he needs to give up his stage management career and come in with us full time. I have to say, he didn't need much persuading to give up his prompt corner. And he is looking forward to growing the business. Everything is turning out fabulously. I made us all cocktails (it is the hit of maraschino liqueur that tips the balance in the G.C. Punch), and then it was on with our hats, lock up shop and celebrate with an early lunch.

First things first. I must order up new flyers and cards. I notice a printer has opened up in the Earl's Court Road.

'Corliss Claflin, writer, lyricist and musical director' – God, what fun.

I wish I did not have such a terrible cough.

DOOR CLOSING

Aunt Tennessee did not live to see the opening night of her musical. Indeed, the musical itself did not make it past the first few opening bars.

Tennie made a last-minute push at further celebrity by dying, unexpectedly, on 18 January 1923, at the home of her grandniece Utica Celestia Welles Beecham, who was married to the conductor Sir Thomas Beecham. (Corliss's first thought on hearing of the location of her demise being, 'Oh, my God, she was hoping for an opera.')

On her death, rumours abounded about the scale of her fortune. Tricky to the end, she had died intestate. The Chicago Tribune *ran with a 'rags to riches' article based around Corliss's brother Albert, valuing the estate at ten million dollars. The brothers Albert, Arthur and Corliss all hoped to share in the predicted millions. In the end the estate passed in its entirety to Aunt Victoria (*the Tribune *reported that the inheritance was now a measly 'seven hundred thousand dollars'). So Albert was forced to continued with his drive to initiate the housewives of America into the joys of the sewing machine. Victoria proudly remained in the starring role until her death.*

Corliss and Marnie had already by this time established themselves and the agency in Bellevue Road, Barnes. Marnie got her telephone, and could be heard proudly answering with the number 'Putney 2121'.

Corliss's cough did not go away. He was advised to seek a warmer climate, which, thanks to various pecuniary advances made by Aunt Tennie before she died, he was able to do. Each autumn The Stage *newspaper would devote a short paragraph to their whereabouts, 'Variety Gossip' informing their readers that Mr and Mrs Claflin had been spotted at Victoria Station en route to The Palace Hotel, Nice. A similar piece would run on their return to London in mid-April.*

Sadly, the 'Continental' aspect of the agency did not last for long. Corliss died in 1932, aged sixty-two. He is buried in East Sheen Cemetery. The headstone on the grave reads 'To my darling husband and pal'.

———ɛ/ɛ/ɛ⸞———

So, what of the house, and the people who take up the space left by Corliss and Marnie?

At this point in history we lose track of the occupants. In 1942 a fire takes place in the Office of Works in Hayes. This completely destroys all the records of the 1931 census. There is a sad report compiled by the inspector of the time, stating that the sight which greeted him was one of complete devastation, and any kind of salvage operation would be useless. (It was concluded that the fire was occasioned not by 'enemy action', but probably by a cigarette carelessly discarded by one of the six fire-guards paid to watch over the office.)

The same inspector shows concern over the 1921 census, which also seems to have suffered. Some schedules were damaged by flooding and were brought in part to Somerset House, where, he reports, they were 'scattered' over various parts of the building (creating a wonderful image of sheets of paper steaming on cast-iron radiators). Whether the records are complete we shall not know until 2022, when the census will be released to the general public.

During the Second World War, the census was not taken.

The house itself had a very narrow escape. A study of the London County Council bomb damage maps shows that a bomb landed on Finborough Road, damaging the houses four doors up beyond all repair. No. 53 suffered general blast damage, but structurally remained sound, waiting to open its doors to the new generation of occupants.

In the 1960s the house remained divided into bed-sits. By the time the author moved in during the early 1980s the house had been subdivided into two completely separate dwellings, sharing a common hallway. At that time, the upper flat was still in multiple occupancy, with three separate bedrooms, two kitchens and a shared bathroom.

The area is still very much 'Little Chelsea', a road on the border, but the house retains the architectural features built to impress the middle classes all those years ago by Mr William Corbett and Mr Alexander McClymont.

The keyholders

THE AUTHOR
AUTUMN 2017

CLARE HASTINGS
Aged sixty-six years, author

I hope I have added to the life of the house.

During the thirty-four years that my partner and I have lived here, we have raised a child, shared the space with more au pairs than was good for us, and heard the arguments, parties, tears and laughter that reverberate through the walls from the people around us. Equally, they have shared in our pleasures and *débâcles*.

That's London for you.

I like to think that a bit of my DNA has been rubbed into the walls, and am hopeful that the business card I pushed through a crack between the floorboards will be found some time in the far future by an excited owner redecorating. I give them full permission to imagine my life in whatever way the fancy takes them, and hope it will give them as much pleasure as cogitating on the previous occupants has given to me.

This is for them.

Author's note

In this book, fact and fiction are intermingled. Although I have used the names, ages and occupations of the house's residents, collected from the census, that is where similarity to the actual people begins and ends. All the characters portrayed are entirely imaginary, and no resemblance to their real selves is or was intended.

I would like to thank house historian Peter Bushell, who set me on the road by collating the documents of provenance. And I want to mention *Earl's Court and Brompton Past* by Richard Tames (Historical Publications Limited, 2000), a book on the area and its residents that is filled with interest.

Finally huge gratitude to all at Pimpernel Press for their enthusiasm and support, especially to Jo Christian, whose 'Oh, Clare . . .' emails are just the inspiration an author needs before sitting down to look at the blank page.

Clare Hastings
5 February 2018